"Emma," He Said Slowly, His Eyes Dark And Solemn As He Stared Into Her Own. "Will You Marry Me?"

Emma had heard of being struck speechless before, but she'd never actually experienced it until this moment.

He'd just asked her to marry him. Mitch. Had asked her. To marry him.

"It may not be a love match," he said, running his hands up her arms to cup her shoulders. "I know that, but we get along well enough to make a marriage work. There's no doubt we're good in bed. And I'll take care of you, no matter what."

Maybe he didn't love her. Maybe he never would. Or maybe he just didn't love her *yet*.

Dear Reader,

There's just something about a cowboy, isn't there? As many of you probably know, I began my publishing career writing Western historical romances, each one exploring a different aspect of that great American icon—the man who wears faded jeans, dusty boots and a well-worn Stetson to perfection. But even though I have since made the transition to the contemporary time period, I'd always hoped for the chance to bring those elements with me into the modern world.

Which is why I'm so excited to share with you *Bedded* Then *Wed,* my first Silhouette Desire book with a cowboy hero. Mitch Ramsey is definitely the strong, silent type, but I think Emma Davis is just the woman to tame him. I hope you'll agree!

And if you have a moment, please drop by my Web site at www.HeidiBetts.com, where you can read about current and upcoming releases, enter contests, chat with other readers on the message board and even blog with me. I'll look forward to seeing you there.

Happy holidays and happy reading!

Heidi Betts

P.S. Doesn't every tall, dark and handsome rancher deserve a sexy younger brother? Watch for Chase Ramsey's story, *Blackmailed into Bed,* coming February 2007!

HEIDI BETTS
BEDDED
THEN WED

Silhouette

Desire

Published by Silhouette Books

America's Publisher of Contemporary Romance

 SILHOUETTE BOOKS

ISBN-13: 978-0-373-76761-8
ISBN-10:   0-373-76761-7

BEDDED *THEN* WED

Copyright © 2006 by Heidi Betts

Visit Silhouette Books at www.eHarlequin.com

Printed in U.S.A.

HEIDI BETTS

An avid romance reader since junior high school, Heidi knew early on that she wanted to write these wonderful stories of love and adventure. It wasn't until her freshman year of college, however, when she spent the entire night reading a romance novel instead of studying for finals, that she decided to take the road less traveled and follow her dream. In addition to reading, writing and romance, she is the founder of her local Romance Writers of America chapter and has a tendency to take injured and homeless animals of every species into her central Pennsylvania home.

Heidi loves to hear from readers. You can write to her at P.O. Box 99, Kylertown, PA 16847 (an SASE is appreciated but not necessary), or e-mail heidi@heidibetts.com. And be sure to visit www.heidibetts.com for news and information about upcoming books.

In loving memory of my cousin, Kathy (Stock) Mulder. A beautiful, caring soul, taken from us much too soon.

And always, for Daddy.

One

The last, slow strains of an old Tammy Wynette song spilled from a small portable radio set up on the steps of the park's gazebo to replace the more elaborate sound system that had been used earlier that evening, and Emma Davis covered her mouth to hide another yawn.

Lord, she was exhausted. She'd spent all yesterday cooking and baking for today's Fourth of July shindig, then most of the morning helping to decorate the town square.

The Gabriel's Crossing holiday celebrations were legendary, and she was more than happy to lend a hand wherever she could. But now, at eleven o'clock at night, she was just plain exhausted. She wanted nothing more than to go home, fall into bed, and sleep for a week…or at least until noon the next day.

Unfortunately, it didn't look like she would get to do any of those things for quite some time yet.

She cast a glance over her shoulder, to where her father and three of his cronies sat at a worn card table, playing what had to be their two-dozenth hand of poker. Unlike Emma—and everyone else, who had pretty much collected their things and headed home hours ago—her father didn't seem anywhere near ready to leave.

With a soft groan, she lowered her head to where her arms rested atop the rough planks of the picnic table and closed her eyes. If she couldn't get to her own bed, then she would sleep right here. At this point, she wasn't particular.

"Need a ride home?"

The low, gravelly voice penetrated her tired brain and she lifted her head to stare up at her neighbor and one of her closest friends since childhood.

Closest friend and secret crush…or at least he had been in high school.

Oh, who was she kidding? Just looking at Mitch Ramsey, with his black-as-sin hair and gray, penetrating eyes, was enough to send the blood pumping through her veins.

A moment ago she'd been so tired she could barely put a single thought together, now she felt wide awake and ready to do the two-step…as long as Mitch was two-stepping right along with her.

When she didn't answer right away, Mitch tapped his beat-up Stetson against the side of his muscular thigh and offered her a kind smile. "Your father seems to be pretty involved in his card game, but you look about ready to drop. Why don't you let me take you home, and he can come along whenever he's ready."

My hero, she thought, and could have sworn her heart skipped a beat.

It had always been that way with Mitch…he smiled and

her belly flip-flopped. He drawled her name, and she felt it all the way down to her toes.

This wasn't the first time he'd come to her rescue, either. Mitch was a gentleman right down to his born-and-bred Texas roots.

"That would be great, thank you." She pushed herself up from the bench seat of the picnic table and brushed her hands on the legs of her jeans. "Let me just go tell Pop I'm leaving."

Mitch gave a small nod, staying where he was while she wandered over to the group of poker buddies.

"Hey, Pop," she said, curling her hands over her father's shoulders and leaning in to kiss his bearded cheek.

Wyatt Davis gave a chuckle, laid out his cards, and said, "Read 'em and weep, boys." His full house clearly beat his friends' hands, and he wasted no time dragging his winnings toward him across the table.

Once he had all the chips in front of him, he turned his head and tipped his face up to Emma. "Hey, there, baby girl. How are you doing?"

"I'm tired and ready to go home." Before his mustachioed mouth could turn down in a frown, she added, "Mitch has offered to take me so you can stick around and play cards as long as you like."

Wyatt glanced past her to where Mitch was standing, fitting his hat on his dark head. "That's awfully nice of him. You sure you don't mind?"

She smiled and gave his shoulders a squeeze. "Of course not. You have fun. No more drinking, though, or we'll have to find someone to drive *you* home, too."

Her father grinned and pointed to the brown bottle to his right. "Don't worry about me, pumpkin, I'll be nursing this one the rest of the night."

"All right." She leaned over and kissed the top of his

head. "See you in the morning. Win big. Bye, guys," she said, waving to her father's friends as she made her way back to Mitch.

"Ready to go?"

She nodded, grabbing her purse from the picnic table and following Mitch to his dark blue truck, shining near-black in the moonlight. He held the door open while she climbed in, then slammed it behind her and walked around to the driver's side. After he'd gotten in behind the wheel and started the engine, he adjusted the air-conditioning to cool the inside of the cab and turned on the radio so that a familiar country tune played in the background.

"Thanks again for this," Emma murmured softly when she realized he didn't intend to carry on a conversation. "I had visions of spending the night curled up on that picnic table. If I'd known Pop planned to stick around playing cards all night, I'd have suggested we take separate cars."

"No problem. I was headed in your direction, anyway." He graced her with a quick grin that creased the corners of his mouth.

"Yeah. If I'd thought of that, I probably would have asked you for a ride hours ago."

Mitch's ranch, the Circle R, bordered her father's property. There were plenty of acres in between, but for all intents and purposes, they were next-door neighbors.

"So, what were you doing hanging around the celebration this late? I'd have expected you to hightail it out of there at the first opportunity."

Mitch was a hometown favorite and more than willing to help out any time Gabriel's Crossing needed him, but ever since his divorce from Suzanne four years earlier, he'd become quiet and withdrawn. He spent most of his time alone on his ranch, going into town only when he needed supplies, or for an event like tonight's—the town's annual Independence Day celebration. But even then, he usually only made a brief appearance before disappearing again, back to the Circle R.

"Chase took Mom home after the fireworks, but since he was in charge of the sound system he needed someone to stick around and dismantle everything." He hitched a thumb over his shoulder, indicating the equipment piled into the truck bed. "I'll have to drop that stuff off in the morning."

"Why didn't you take your mother home?" she pressed, knowing that would have been Mitch's choice over staying to the very end of the town-wide party.

Even from where she was sitting, on the opposite side of the bench seat, she could see the wry twist of his lips.

"Because my family thinks I'm becoming a hermit and need to get out more. And that if I stuck around long enough tonight, I might have met a nice girl and gotten married again."

His tone told her how enamored he was of that idea, but she couldn't help the tiny flicker of awareness that bloomed to life inside her.

She opened her mouth to speak, then had to clear her throat before she thought the words would come out as more than a squeak. "Did you? Meet a nice girl, I mean."

"No," he answered without reservation, and with the slightest hint of an edge to his voice. "But then, I wasn't looking for one."

The flicker in her belly sputtered and died. She shouldn't be surprised. It was no secret that Suzanne's infidelities and the divorce had hit him hard. He'd never been the most outgoing guy to begin with, but after the divorce he'd become noticeably more sullen. Nothing anyone said or did seemed to shake his sour mood.

And he had never looked at her as anything other than a neighbor and friend—no matter how much she might wish he would.

Not that she'd ever done anything about it. She could have flirted a little, or come right out and told him she had the hots for him. Instead, she'd kept her feelings to herself while pining after him from afar.

She was such a coward. Maybe if she hadn't been, he wouldn't have married Suzanne in the first place and wouldn't be so miserable now.

Swallowing uncomfortably, she rubbed her palms along the tops of her jean-clad legs and breathed a sigh of relief when she realized they were nearing her house. Getting home would mean an end to the awkward silence filling the cab.

Mitch pulled up in front of the pale yellow, ranch-style house and cut the engine.

"You want me to walk you to the door?"

Considering the walk would take all of about two seconds and ten steps, it was a gracious but unnecessary offer.

"Thanks, but I need to check the livestock one last time before I go to bed, anyway."

She released the latch on her seatbelt and opened the passenger side door. When she turned from closing it, she was surprised to find Mitch moving toward her in that long, lanky stride of his.

"What are you doing?" she asked, her mind drawing a complete blank as to why he'd bothered to get out of the truck at all.

"Helping you with the livestock."

"That's all right, I can handle it." It might not be her favorite pastime, but she'd grown up pitching hay, mucking stalls and grooming horses, and—along with several ranch hands—still helped her father on a daily basis. Checking water buckets and tossing out a little extra grain by herself would be child's play.

"I know you can," he told her, catching an arm around her shoulders. "But things will go faster and you'll be able to get to bed quicker if we both do the work."

She couldn't argue with his logic, so she said nothing as they made their way across the grass-sprigged dirt yard to the big gray barn.

One half of the large double doors was propped open. They walked inside, and Emma flipped a switch to her left to turn on the lights. The uncovered bulbs dangling high above their heads weren't very bright but illuminated enough of the building so that they could see what they were doing.

Mitch had spent so much time at the Double D as a child that he knew where everything was. The horses nickered at the interruption to their rest, and Mitch patted more than one equine nose as they passed.

While she shook a bit of fresh hay into each horse's feed trough and checked to make sure they had clean water, Mitch hauled a bale outside. She knew he would carry the hay out a ways into the field, then spread it on the ground for the cattle to find during the night.

They finished at nearly the same time. She was wiping her hands on the seat of her jeans when he strolled back in, the leftover baling twine clutched in one hand. He hung the strings on a nail sticking out of a nearby beam, then turned to face her, hands on hips.

"All done?" he wanted to know.

"Just about." Moving farther into the wide open space of the barn, she wrapped her fingers around the sides of the ladder that led to the loft and said, "I want to check on a new litter of kittens before we leave."

She scurried up the ladder in a matter of seconds,

creeping quietly across the straw-strewn floor in search of the kittens. The light up here was even weaker than down below, but she could still make out the shapes of stray bales and—hopefully—tiny bundles of fur.

A second later, a board squeaked behind her and she turned her head to see Mitch standing at the top of the ladder. Her stomach did another one of those queer flip-flops at the sight of him, then settled down to a dull simmer.

"You didn't have to come up," she whispered.

"I wanted to," he said just as softly, but didn't elaborate.

Deciding Mitch pretty much did what he wanted, whenever he wanted, she went back to looking for the kittens. She found them tucked together in a tight ball, nestled into a pile of loose straw in the corner. They were adorable, and so small she thought she could probably hold the entire brood of them in the palms of both hands.

There were five in total—two tabbies, one calico, one white, and one black with white feet and a streak of white on its nose. She'd been playing with them on an almost daily basis since she'd discovered them. They were old enough that their eyes were open but young enough that they still wobbled when they tried to walk.

Not wanting to disturb their rest, she intended to simply back away and leave them be, but then the mama cat appeared, rubbing between Emma's legs before moving to her babies and lying down to let them feed. They immediately woke up and started nuzzling around their mother's belly, and Emma took the opportunity to stroke their soft little heads and backs.

Most barn cats were afraid of people because they didn't get handled as much as house cats, but from the time she was old enough to toddle around in her father's footsteps, Emma had loved the odd collection of felines running around the property. Her father used to tell her to be careful or she'd stroke them all bald, but so far that hadn't happened. Instead, they had a barn full of friendly cats that often came running when they heard the doors open and would pester for attention while you were trying to work.

"Cute," Mitch murmured just above her left ear, startling her.

She straightened, covering her heart with her hand. For a moment, she'd forgotten he was there but wondered now how she ever could have made such a grievous error. His tall frame and broad shoulders filled the space around them like a sponge in a glass of water. His presence alone seemed to suck all the oxygen out of the air and make her short of breath.

"Well," she said nervously, backing a step or two away, "I just wanted to see how they were doing. We can leave now."

Instead of heading for the ladder to climb back to the main floor of the barn, Mitch moseyed over to a couple of bales of straw stacked against the far wall and sat down.

"What's your hurry?" he asked, leaning back on his elbows until he was nearly lying flat. "If we wait for the kittens to fill their bellies, you might get to pet them again."

Stuffing her hands into the hip pockets of her jeans, she rocked back on her heels. She could play with the kittens anytime, which he probably knew perfectly well. But he seemed to want to hang around a while longer, and she didn't get the chance to talk to him very often anymore, especially alone. Besides, as tired as she'd been only half an hour ago at the picnic area, she didn't feel at all sleepy now.

Feet dragging slightly through the loose straw that covered the loft floor, she took a seat beside him. She kept her spine straight, her hands on her knees as she searched for something to say. The problem was, she'd already exhausted her list of small-talk topics on the drive home. She didn't have a clue what else to say that wouldn't sound forced or too probing into his personal life.

Thankfully, Mitch kept the moment from turning awkward.

"So how'd you enjoy the celebration today?"

"It was fine," she said. "The Fourth of July picnic is always fun."

"Yeah." He picked up a long strand of golden-yellow straw and twirled it between two fingers, casting shadows in the dim light. "I got a slice of your cherry pie before it was all gone. It was good."

"Thanks."

"You made some of the other food, too, right? I thought I heard somebody mention you always cook a lot for the picnic."

She nodded, remembering all the times she, Mitch and his brother, Chase, had hung out together just like this. On those long summer days when it was too hot to run or play, they'd found a shady spot to do nothing more than lie around and shoot the breeze. The happy childhood memories eased her nerves and she began to relax.

"Mom used to cook up a storm for all the town celebrations, you know. After she died, I guess I picked up where she left off. I had her recipes, and I didn't want anyone to be disappointed."

"I think people would have understood," he said seriously.

"Probably. But I enjoy it, and I think it makes Pop feel more like Mom's still around."

"She did make the best potato salad in Texas."

"Yes, she did," Emma agreed with a smile.

"Yours was pretty tasty, too."

She met his storm-gray eyes and grinned. "How do you

know it was my potato salad you were eating?" There had to have been at least four or five bowls of the stuff, all prepared by different cooks.

He sat up and leaned closer to her, one corner of his mouth quirked with amusement. "Because I saw you arrive and watched you set the bowl on the table with the rest of the food. Then I made sure to get there early before it was all gone."

His face was inches from her own, hovering over her, smelling of some crisp, clean aftershave she couldn't quite identify. Whatever it was, it made her think of waking up in the arms of a strong, sexy man. This man, in particular. Running her fingers over his stubbled, unshaven jaw... kissing his warm, pale lips...feeling the full, bare length of him pressed against her while they slowly stirred each other's arousal.

"I didn't see you," she responded quietly, unable to tear her gaze from his tempting mouth. "Not until much later."

"I was hiding out to avoid those nosy questions I get whenever I show my face in town. But I could still see every move you made."

She shivered with awareness at his words. He'd been watching her at the picnic and she hadn't even known it.

Instead of feeling unnerved that he'd essentially been spying on her all day, she was flattered...and suddenly incredibly turned on.

"I wish I'd known you were there," she said, boldly lifting her hand to caress the strong line of his jaw. "I would have asked you to dance."

He wrapped his fingers around hers, pulling her hand away from his face and turning it to press a kiss to the center of her palm. Tiny flames of desire flickered to life in her belly and started to spread outward.

"We could dance now," he offered softly.

She shook her head. "There's no music."

"I don't know," he murmured, brushing her bottom lip with the pad of his thumb, "I definitely hear something in the air."

And then he leaned forward, covering her mouth with his own.

Emma's heart kicked up, pounding in her chest like the hooves of a galloping horse. Mitch Ramsey was kissing her. Finally. Gloriously.

His lips were firm, skillful. He knew exactly where to press, where to move, when to open his mouth and encourage her to do the same. While his tongue darted over and around hers, she tasted the coffee with just a touch of cream and sugar that he must have drank before bringing her home.

Her nipples turned hard and pressed against the inside cups of her bra as he stroked her from hip to breast. The heat of his touch burned through her blouse, raising goose bumps along her flesh and sending her core temperature soaring.

She ran her hands over his back, feeling the sleek muscles beneath his shirt, the way they rippled and flexed as he moved. Using her nails like claws, she tore at the tail of his shirt, dragging it out from the waistband of his jeans until the pads of her fingers encountered smooth, bare skin.

Between them, he was loosening the buttons of her blouse from top to bottom, opening her to the night air. And Emma let him...more than let him. She moved however she thought was needed to grant him the best access.

It was amazing, wonderful, spectacular. Everything she'd ever imagined and more.

She was panting for breath when Mitch grasped her shoulders and pushed her slightly away. His own chest heaved as he stared down at her, his eyes dark with desire.

"Don't stop," she blurted out, thrusting her fingers into the hair at his temples and drawing him near once again.

She was so afraid he'd stop. So afraid the tight line of his lips meant he was about to apologize and say that kissing her was a mistake.

But it wasn't a mistake; it was what she wanted. Had wanted, more than anything, for years.

"Please," she said again, more softly this time, uncaring that she likely sounded desperate and pathetic, "don't stop."

"Not a chance," he murmured, just before he lowered his head to kiss her again and sent her world back to the realm of temporary perfection.

Two

Mitch's body was on fire, throbbing with need and straining to get closer to Emma.

Four years. It had been four years since his divorce from Suzanne and four *long* years since he'd been with a woman. The time had taken its toll and stretched his control to the breaking point.

And now here he was, with a warm and willing woman in his arms.

Never mind that it was Emma, childhood friend and neighbor, a woman he shouldn't even be contemplating sleeping with.

But she tasted like peppermint and smelled like flowers and reminded him of a time in his life when he hadn't been miserable. Back when they were kids, without a care in the world, when he was first married to Suzanne, head over heels in love and believing they would always be that way.

Emma was safe and familiar…and sexy as all get out.

How had he never noticed that before? The way her small, firm breasts filled out the front of her blouse and her soft lips formed a seductive little moue. Or the way her strawberry-blond hair fell to her shoulders and perfectly framed her heart-shaped face.

He shouldn't be thinking of her in those terms, shouldn't be touching and kissing her. But she felt so good, so right, he couldn't seem to stop.

She made soft mewling sounds as their tongues tangled and her body writhed against his. He pushed her shirt the rest of the way off her shoulders, letting it fall to the bale of straw behind her.

Her chest rose and fell with her breathing, as rapidly as his own. But he didn't let it keep him from sliding his right hand over her left breast, beneath the lacy material of her bra. His fingers caressed the pillowy softness while his thumb teased and flicked the hardened nipple.

She moaned in pleasure, sending shockwaves rippling through his bloodstream. Her head fell back, exposing the long, smooth column of her throat, and he couldn't resist kissing her there, licking the pulse point and nibbling at the taut line of muscle.

He used his free hand to unhook the latch of her bra and skim the loosened straps down her arms.

In the back of his mind, he hoped she would protest. If she asked him to stop, suffered a sudden bout of embarrassment, he was gentleman enough not to pressure her to go farther than she felt comfortable. But on his own…

On his own, he wasn't sure he was man enough to let her go.

He had full access now to her bare chest and took a moment to admire the pale splendor of her small, pert breasts with their tiny cherry nipples. They reminded him of ice cream sundaes, sweet and delectable and good enough to eat.

Shifting around on the bales of straw, he supported her back with one arm while leaning in for a taste. He kissed the side of her breast, then opened his mouth to sample the silken skin.

She raked her hands through his hair, grazing the scalp and anchoring her fingers near his nape. His tongue drew circles around her tightened areola, the movements growing smaller and smaller until he engulfed the entire tip.

She straddled his thighs like a champion rider, tilting her hips, straining for a more intimate touch. And he wanted to give it to her, was desperate for it himself. Sweating, shaking, more aroused than he could ever remember being before in his life.

Releasing her breast, dragging in great gulps of air, he returned his mouth to her lips. At the same time, he tried to get his trembling fingers to work on the snap and zipper of her jeans.

With the denim loose around her waist, he slipped his hands inside, palms flat against her skin as he slid them down, beneath the elastic edge of her panties. He skimmed her hips, then moved around to cup her buttocks.

When she moaned and ground herself into the hard bulge behind the zipper of his own jeans, he knew he couldn't wait much longer to be inside her. Not without embarrassing himself and depriving them both of something he was beginning to suspect would be earth-shattering.

Laying her back along the bed of straw bales, he sat up only long enough to yank off her shoes and drag her pants down her legs. Then he was with her again, tearing off his shirt, unbuckling his belt and opening his fly before covering her with his body.

He lifted her legs around his waist, gently probing her warm, moist folds. Brushing thin strands of strawberry-blond hair away from her face, he met her eyes and offered her an encouraging smile. She returned his grin and lifted her hands to his shoulders, applying just enough pressure to tug him down for a kiss. While his tongue plumbed the depths of her mouth, he cocked his hips and entered her in one long, strong stroke.

The instant friction and intense sensation made them both gasp. Mitch held himself perfectly still, feeling her tight inner muscles flexing around him, all but blowing off the top of his head. He knew if he moved, if she shifted even a millimeter, things between them would be over much too soon.

So he gritted his teeth, concentrating on his breathing until the blaze in his gut sputtered to a low forest fire and he thought he could open his eyes, gaze down at Emma's angelic features without exploding. She was staring up at him with liquid blue eyes, the same stunned expression on her face that he suspected mirrored his own.

Taking a deep breath, he let the air shudder out of his lungs, and then brushed his lips across her mouth.

Her breasts brushed his chest, her arms and legs locked around him like tentacles. With a minor shift, just a small forward movement, he was inside her, buried to the hilt.

He groaned, the sound rumbling up from his diaphragm even as she flexed around him and he began to move. Short, slow strokes growing slightly longer and faster as the tension built. Blood pumped through his veins, hot and flowing like molten lava to pool between his legs.

Emma threw her head back and he kissed her throat,

nibbled her ear, trailed his lips down to her breasts. His belly clenched at the noises she was making. Low, erotic mewling sounds that drove him senseless and made him thrust harder, faster, striving for completion.

Sweat dripped past his temples and down the middle of his back. Her fingers tangled in his hair, caressing and keeping him close as her hips rose and fell to meet him.

"Emma," he growled out.

She met his gaze and smiled even as her mouth opened on a rush of ecstasy. "Mitch," she breathed in return.

And that was all it took to send him over the edge. White-hot pleasure pounded through his pores, filling every cell of his being to near bursting.

With a deep groan, he drove into her one last time, relieved to feel her pulse and shake, following him over the cliff into mindless pleasure.

Emma couldn't keep her lips from curling up in a grin as she ran her hands over Mitch's silky-soft hair and sweat-slickened back, his strong, muscular bicep and broad chest.

His face rested in the hollow of her neck, his body still covering hers after the most intense session of lovemaking she'd ever experienced.

She still couldn't believe it had happened. Her body hummed with recently released passion, the lingering effects causing her muscles to twitch and a delightful warmth to spread all over.

And she knew, without a shadow of a doubt, that with anyone but Mitch Ramsey, the sex might have been good, but it wouldn't have been phenomenal.

So many times, private wishes and forbidden fantasies lost their luster in the bright light of day. She'd dreamed of being with Mitch for so long that when he'd begun to kiss her, a part of her had been worried she'd be disappointed.

Or perhaps she'd been worried that she would disappoint him.

Instead, being with him had been everything she'd hoped for and more. So much more.

He'd been gentle and caring and…amazing. Not only in the way he touched her—although the memory of that alone was enough to curl her toes and cause a renewed warmth to pool deep in her belly.

No, he'd been kind and considerate all evening. Offering her a ride home, helping her tend to the livestock, climbing into the loft with her to check on the kittens.

It was a side of him she hadn't seen in a very long time. Since Suzanne had ripped his heart out and stomped it into the ground, leaving him an empty husk of his former self.

Mitch thought he'd handled his ex-wife's infidelity and the subsequent divorce well. He thought he'd been impervious to the pain that woman had caused him and had recovered quickly to return to his normal life.

But everyone around him knew it was a lie. He pretended to be okay while his insides remained shriveled and cold.

Emma often thought that if she ever ran into Suzanne again, she would slap the cheating bitch for what she'd done to Mitch.

But then, Emma had never liked the woman. From the moment Mitch had brought her home to Gabriel's Crossing, having met her at a truck stop in Abilene, Emma had known that every dream she'd ever had of spending her life with Mitch was destroyed.

Suzanne was tall and blond and built like a 1920s pin-up girl, while Emma had always had a more boyish figure. Small breasts, narrow hips, no feminine curves to speak of.

She was a bit of a tomboy, and had always been proud of the fact, until Suzanne Yates had waltzed into town and reminded her of all the things she wasn't, stealing Mitch in the process.

It had been a silly dream to start with, thinking that just because she and Mitch had grown up together he might fall in love with her. She'd grown up with Chase, too, but had never had an erotic or ever-after thought about him.

And until tonight, she'd truly thought she was over Mitch Ramsey. Or, if not over him, at least had come to terms with the fact that he was never going to completely heal from Suzanne's betrayal. He was off the market and more out of her reach than ever before.

Now, though, she wasn't sure what to think. Her heart wanted to believe this was the start of something permanent. That by driving her home tonight and making love to her in the barn loft, he was showing that he was recovered from his lousy marriage and willing to love again.

But her rational, more somber brain warned her to be careful. Reminded her that one night of passion did not a marriage proposal make.

She would keep that in mind, play it safe and follow his lead, whatever it may be.

"Mmm." He moaned low in his throat like a man waking from a good night's sleep and pushed himself up on one elbow.

Cool night air washed over her skin where his body no longer covered, and she fought not to shiver. Not because she was cold, but because she missed the intimate contact.

"You okay?" he asked, still leaning over her, staring down at her with those slate-gray eyes.

She nodded, biting the inside of her lip to keep from saying more.

He shifted again, rolling farther away on the bales of straw. She felt bereft without his touch, but curled her fingers into fists at her sides and took deep breaths until she got the urge to reach for him under control.

"We should think about getting dressed before your father gets home and catches us out here." He shot her a wicked grin. "I've made it almost forty years without getting chased off by an angry, pitch fork-wielding father. There's no sense in starting now."

Moving around her, he climbed to his feet and began gathering their discarded clothes from the straw-strewn floor. She sat up and accepted her things when he handed them to her, taking her time putting bra and panties then her jeans and blouse back on.

She ran her hands through her hair, picking out pieces of straw and wishing for a brush to smooth the tangled mass. When she looked back at Mitch, he was dressed and just fastening his belt.

When he was finished, he slapped his hands against his thighs and fixed her with a lopsided smile. "Should we head down?"

She glanced around, surprised to find no visible signs of what had happened between them. After their explosive joining, she'd expected to see burn marks, singed straw, smoke still rising from the ashes. But, instead, there was just plain yellow straw, a little flat in places, but ordinary enough, and the litter of kittens curled up sleeping around their mother.

Turning back to meet his gaze, she nodded, then climbed down the ladder ahead of him.

Just as they reached the door of the barn, they heard tires crunching on the dirt and gravel drive, and saw headlights headed their way.

"That'll be Pop," she told him.

"Looks like we made it just in time." He stuck his hands in the front pockets of his jeans, his thumbs hooked over his belt and waistband.

If he was nervous about coming face-to-face with her father only minutes after having her naked and writhing beneath him, he didn't show it.

Her father pulled his pickup into the yard and cut the engine. A second later, the door opened and he climbed out.

He didn't look completely steady on his feet, and she rushed forward to take his arm, hoping he'd kept his word about only finishing off that one last beer.

His head snapped up when he felt her hand on his elbow, and he smiled through his shaggy gray beard and mustache.

"Well, there you are. I thought you would have been in the house, asleep by now. What are you doing out here?"

"Mitch and I were just…um…"

"Checking the livestock," Mitch offered, stepping out of the shadows of the barn and into the glow of the house's front porch light.

"Good, good," her father said. "Thanks for helping out my girl, Ramsey."

Emma's cheeks heated, but she hoped neither her father nor Mitch would notice in the dark.

"My pleasure, sir," Mitch answered, rocking back on the heels of his well-worn boots, hands still in his pockets. "Anything else I can do for you tonight before I get going?"

"No, no, you go on." Her father started toward the house, slipping out of Emma's hold and looking more steady on his feet now that he'd had the chance to stand for a few minutes. "Have a good night. We'll see you soon."

"Yes, sir. Good night, sir."

"Emma, I'm going to bed. I'll see you in the morning."

"All right. 'Night, Pop. I love you."

"Love you, too, sweetheart."

The screen door slammed closed behind him and she waited several long seconds before speaking. Once she was sure he was out of earshot, she turned to face Mitch.

"Went a little overboard with the 'yes, sir,' 'no, sir,' 'have a good night, sirs,' didn't you?"

She thought she saw him wince and bit back a chuckle of amusement.

"Maybe," he answered shortly, his face a mask of inexpression. "But it sure beats the alternative."

"What's that?"

"Letting him know I spent the last half hour rolling around in the loft with his daughter."

It was Emma's turn to wince, and she cast a quick glance over her shoulder, afraid her father might have been close enough to overhear Mitch's declaration.

She was a grown woman, so what she did with her body and with whom was no one's business but her own. But talking about sex in front of her father—or worse, having him know she'd just finished having hot, extremely satisfying sex in his barn—was still something that made her keenly uncomfortable.

"Point taken."

Gravel crunched beneath her feet as she crossed to him, then followed as he stalked to his truck.

"Thanks for your help with the horses and cattle," she said.

He nodded, opening the door and climbing inside.

Watching him get ready to leave made her stomach clench. But what had she expected? That he would ask to stay the night or suggest they sneak back into the barn for seconds? That he would declare his undying love and fall to one knee, asking her to marry him?

She might harbor fantasies of happily-ever-after with him, but she wasn't delusional. She was realistic enough to accept that sex was just sex, even if it had been with the one man she'd always secretly had a crush on.

"So I guess I'll see you around," she offered. The perfect opening for him to ask her out on a date, tell her he'd call, anything to imply that what had passed between them would be more than a one-night stand.

"Yeah," he replied, and nothing more.

A beat passed before he started the engine, then turned his head to meet her gaze. "'Night."

Forcing a smile to her lips, she swallowed back the bubble of disappointment swelling in her belly. "Right. Good night."

He put the truck in gear, turned around and rolled slowly down the drive. She stood watching until his taillights disappeared, rubbing her arms to stave off a chill that centered in her chest and had nothing to do with the still night air surrounding her.

Three

Emma glanced at her shopping list. She had everything she needed except bread flour.

Turning down the baking aisle, she scanned the shelves for the brand and type she wanted, groaning when she spotted it on the uppermost shelf. The store had apparently rearranged items since the last time she'd purchased bread flour. And at five foot three, that left it just a couple of inches out of her range.

Pushing her cart to the side, she used the toe of her shoe to nudge cans of pie filling on the lowest shelf out of the way, then grabbed hold of a shelf at waist level and hoisted herself up. Her fingertips brushed the front of the bag, but she still couldn't get a good enough grip to lift it down.

"Need some help?"

With a yelp, her hold on the shelf slipped and she fell

backward. Strong hands and an even stronger chest caught and steadied her.

She turned, looking up into Mitch's hard, gray eyes. Not that she'd needed to see him to know who'd spoken to her. She would know his voice anywhere.

"Hey," she greeted him, feeling slightly out of breath, and not because of her graceless pirouette from the grocery store shelves.

It had been two weeks since the Fourth of July picnic, since that night in the barn. Two weeks without seeing or even hearing from him again.

She hadn't been surprised. She would have been more surprised if he'd called or shown up on the doorstep, but that didn't mean she wasn't disappointed.

Disappointed that he could walk away without a backward glance after what they'd shared but also that their sleeping together might have ruined a perfectly good, lifelong friendship.

And now here he stood, staring at her from beneath the rim of his black Stetson. He didn't seem particularly pleased to see her, but then Mitch hadn't looked happy since Suzanne had left. A thin layer of stubble shadowed his square jaw, and lines bracketed his flat mouth.

"Hey, yourself. Is this what you were after?" He reached up with one hand and plucked a bag of bread flour from the top shelf with ease, holding it out to her.

She took it, cradling the five-pound weight to her chest while she swallowed and tried to think of something witty to say to break the tension and attempt to return them to the easy camaraderie they'd shared before sex had muddied the waters.

"You headed somewhere after this?" he asked without preliminaries.

"Just home to put groceries away," she answered.

"Got time for a cup of coffee? Maybe a bite to eat?"

She glanced over her shoulder into the basket of her cart. Nothing cold. Nothing that would go bad if she didn't go straight home.

Her stomach gave a little lurch at the possibilities of what he might want to talk about, but she nodded. "I guess that would be all right."

"Good. Need anything else?"

She checked her list one last time, then shook her head. "No, I'm ready."

They moved down the aisle together, Emma pushing the cart as Mitch followed a step behind. The heels of his boots clicked rhythmically on the hard, tiled floor, matching the nervous beat of her heart.

He stayed with her while she went through the checkout line, then helped to carry the bags to her car.

"Where are we going?" she asked, standing in the open driver's side door.

"Rosie's Café." He tipped his hat down a fraction to shield his eyes from the midday sun. "I'll meet you over there."

Ten minutes later, they were seated across from one another in a red vinyl booth near the back of the café. Located in the center of town, Rosie's was Gabriel's Crossing's most popular restaurant. A greasy spoon where folks came for home cooking and the latest gossip.

The lunch crowd had cleared out already, and dinner customers wouldn't begin to trickle in for a few more hours. When the waitress came, they asked for pie and coffee, then sat in uncomfortable silence while the young woman went to fill their order.

Emma folded and refolded her napkin until the paper edges began to flake and fall away. Finally, she took a deep breath, laid her palms flat on the Formica tabletop, and faced Mitch head-on.

"So, what did you want to talk about?" she blurted out, deciding it was better to simply come to the point than sit here imagining worst case scenarios. Like tearing off a Band-Aid in one quick swipe rather than toying and tugging and prolonging the agony.

"Us."

As much as she'd braced herself for his answer, she hadn't expected that.

She waited until the waitress set slices of pie and steaming cups of black coffee in front of them before responding, using the much-needed time to calm her erratic pulse and get her scattered thoughts in order. He took a sip of black coffee while she stirred a sugar packet and dollop of cream into hers.

Once they were alone, she took a deep breath and kept her tone low so no one would overhear. "What about us?"

"I think there should be one."

She knit her eyebrows. Mitch had never been the easiest man to talk to, but at the moment he was giving new meaning to the word *confusing*. "One what?"

"Us. I think there should be an us."

Picking up his fork, he dug into his slice of blueberry pie as though they were talking about the weather instead of…them.

Before she could reply, he swallowed and went on. "You know what happened between us, Emma. It shouldn't have. It shouldn't have happened the way it did, and for that I'm sorry."

The flush of embarrassment she'd felt at his mention of the night they'd made love flared into sudden anger and more than a little hurt.

How dare he apologize to her for what she considered one of the most special nights of her life? If he was sorry, if he regretted what they'd done, then he should have kept it to himself instead of cornering her like this.

"That's what you brought me here to tell me?" she demanded, her knuckles turning white as she clutched the edge of the table. "You're sorry we slept together? I hate to break it to you, Mitch, but you're not the first man I've had sex with. You didn't seduce me, you didn't take my virginity, you didn't do anything that requires an apology. I'm a big girl. I can make my own decisions and sleep with whomever I want. I don't need your permission or your approval."

A beat passed while he held her gaze, then he nodded. "You're right. You can make your own decisions."

He took another bite of pie and washed it down with a gulp of coffee. "The thing is, I'm not the type to have a one-night stand with a neighbor and childhood friend. It feels…sleazy."

Her eyes narrowed in warning. He wasn't calling her sleazy or even what had passed between them, she knew that. But it was a close thing, and in her current mood she wasn't sure she was willing to split hairs.

"My point is," he continued, "I think maybe we should keep seeing each other. See where it leads."

Of all the things he might have said, that shocked her the most. It also made her heartbeat—which had slowed to a crawl at the direction the conversation was taking— speed up and thump against her rib cage.

She swallowed hard, praying she wasn't hearing things. "Excuse me?"

"I think we should…date. Go out a couple of times and see what happens."

It was half-true, anyway. But the suggestion wasn't driven by interest as much as nobility. And, he admitted, guilt.

In the two weeks since the Fourth of July picnic…since they'd made love in the loft of her father's barn…he hadn't been able to stop thinking about her.

Partly because the sex had been incredible and every fiber of his being wanted to be with her again. And partly because she was his neighbor, a friend since childhood. They'd gone through school together. Climbed trees and ridden horses together. Survived the prom and graduation and the death of a parent—her mother, who had been a second mother to him as well—together.

She wasn't some casual acquaintance to be used to slake his lust. Even if it had been four long, lonely years since he'd been with a woman.

So far, this was the best solution he could come up with. His personal code of honor wouldn't allow him to just walk away and pretend that night had never happened. That might be all right for a stranger he'd met in a bar, but he couldn't treat Emma that way.

Emma deserved better.

Using her for a one-night stand was unacceptable. But dating her for a while wasn't.

Nothing would come of it, he knew. Nothing could ever come of it, and he didn't want it to. But if they dated for a while and then split up, he could justify having slept with her.

And he wouldn't sleep with her again, that was a promise.

Even if the memory of kissing her, touching her soft skin, heated his blood and tightened his trousers across his groin.

He'd known Emma all his life, but this was the first time he'd been distracted by her as a woman. The first time he'd noticed how sexy and attractive she was.

Physically, she was the opposite of Suzanne in every

way. Where Suzanne had an hourglass figure, with full breasts and wide hips, Emma was proportionally well-balanced. Small, but still shapely.

Her hair was more strawberry-blond than peroxide-blond; her look more natural than painted on; her clothes stylish but comfortable, rather than skin-tight and meant to attract attention.

She certainly had succeeded at catching his attention, and not a day went by that he didn't regret it.

"So?" He took a swig of coffee to wash down the last of his pie, taking note that Emma had yet to touch hers. "What do you say?"

What could she say? What *should* she say?

This had to be the most bizarre date invitation she'd ever received. And if it were coming from anyone other than Mitch, she'd have probably laughed the poor guy out of the restaurant.

But it *was* Mitch, which left her torn.

Did she accept because her feminine heart had dreamed of this moment a million times? Or did she turn him down because she suspected the offer stemmed more from guilt than an actual interest in seeing her socially?

Wrapping her fingers around the mug of still-warm coffee in front of her, she lifted it to her mouth and took a sip, buying herself a little more time.

But in the end, she knew what her decision would be. Knew that her heart and her sense of possibility would drive her to at least see where things could lead.

Maybe it would lead only to a couple of dates, dinner or a movie. Or maybe it would lead to more—to Mitch realizing he'd never belonged with Suzanne, but with a woman more like Emma. If she was lucky, with Emma herself.

The sensible side of her brain knew it was too much to

hope for, but she was willing to take a chance. It was a small one, after all, and if things did work out, the payoff would be big. Everything she'd ever dreamed of.

And if it didn't, she was the only person who would ever know her wishes had been for more than a casual relationship. She was the only one who would be hurt.

Taking a deep breath, she returned the cup to its saucer, then lifted her eyes to his. "All right."

"Good." He shifted in the booth, digging his wallet out of his hip pocket, peeling off bills and dropping them onto the tabletop. Then he slid out and got to his feet. "I'll pick you up at six."

Without a backward glance, he stalked out of the diner, leaving her alone with her coffee and uneaten pie.

If she were smart, she told herself for the fiftieth time, she would have called Mitch up and told him to forget about tonight.

He hadn't exactly acted like Prince Charming back at Rosie's when he'd walked out on her. And he hadn't *asked* her out tonight, so much as *told* her when to be ready. For that alone, he almost deserved to be stood up.

Yet here she was, poised in front of her full-length mirror, checking her appearance one last time before he arrived.

She'd already fixed a supper plate for Pop and warned him she would be gone for the evening. She had no idea where Mitch intended to take her, but she assumed dinner would be involved, so she hadn't bothered eating herself.

Then she'd come upstairs and torn apart her closet in search of something decent to wear. Without a destination in mind, it made dressing difficult, but she'd finally settled on a denim skirt and pale-yellow peasant blouse.

Looking at her reflection now, she adjusted the gold

chain at her neck and tucked back a few thin strands of hair that had slipped out of its clip.

Through the open bedroom window, she heard Mitch's truck pull up to the house and her father's greeting as Mitch got out, slamming the door behind him.

She took a deep breath, straightened the hem of her top, then slid her feet into the black mules she'd pulled out of her closet earlier. Regardless of the butterflies tap-dancing through her belly, she'd agreed to go out with him. Beneath the layers of nerves that had her all but jumping out of her skin, she was even looking forward to it.

"Emma, honey," her father shouted up the stairs. "Mitch is here."

As though she wasn't already keenly aware of his presence. Her arms had broken out in gooseflesh the minute he'd turned into the drive.

"Coming," she called, when she found her voice.

He was waiting just inside the kitchen, near the front door. His black Stetson was in his hand rather than on his head, tapping against the side of his denim-clad thigh.

"Hi," she said when his gaze lifted to hers.

"Hi." He scanned her from head to toe, then met her eyes again. "You look nice."

As compliments went, it wasn't the best she'd ever received, but knowing that Mitch didn't dole them out very often to anyone, she decided to accept.

"Thank you. You, too."

He was dressed in jeans and a plaid button-down shirt, the same as usual, but he always looked good to her, so the compliment still fit.

"Ready to go?"

She nodded, grabbing a light jacket from the coatrack beside the door.

"You two have a good time," her father called out from his seat at the kitchen table. He waved them off, barely sparing them a second glance as he dug into his dinner.

Mitch closed the door behind them, then walked her to the passenger side of his truck and helped her climb in.

"So, where are we going?" she asked once he was behind the wheel and they were headed down the long dirt driveway to the main road.

"You'll see."

She raised an eyebrow at his less than enlightening answer, but he kept his eyes on the road and couldn't see the look of consternation she shot him.

Ten minutes later, they pulled into the parking lot of the Silver Spur, one of the most popular honky-tonks in Gabriel's Crossing. Lights blinked on the roof and bright neon signs shone in the windows, advertising a dozen different brands of draft and bottled beer.

Emma had only been to the Spur a couple of times before and always with a group of friends because the bar tended to get rowdy on the weekends. But this was a weeknight, and even though it was a strange place to go for a first date, she was with Mitch, so she had nothing to worry about.

He came around to help her down from the truck, then held her hand as they walked into the bar. Loud country music blared, filling the early evening air and hitting them like an ocean wave when they pushed open the front door.

Men and women, most wearing cowboy hats of all sizes and colors, filled the wide, open room. Dancing, milling around, sitting at the tables and bar with longneck bottles of beer and bowls of peanuts in front of them.

Sawdust was scattered in clumps across the scarred wood floor, and antlers decorated the walls, along with a dartboard and assorted alcoholic beverage posters and signs. At the far end of the room, a live band played on a raised stage and a group of people—mostly made up of couples—line danced to the tune of a Texas two-step.

"So, what do you want to do first?" Mitch asked, leaning over her shoulder and speaking close to her ear to be heard over the volume of the music. "Dance, find a table and order some nachos, or sit at the bar and order a drink?"

She scanned the crowd, weighing her options. This was a far cry from the movie or dinner at a quiet restaurant she'd expected of tonight, but it could still be fun.

"Let's get a drink," she yelled back, tipping her head toward the bar.

With his hand at her back, Emma eased her way through the crush of bodies and hopped up on one of the tall stools lining the long mahogany bar. Mitch took a seat beside her and ordered two cold beers.

Since she hadn't had anything to eat yet that evening, she sipped her drink slowly and tried to avoid their images in the mirror that lined the wall behind the bar.

It wasn't her reflection that made her uncomfortable, but Mitch's. He was too darn handsome, too tall and sinewy and masculine in all the right places.

Beneath the wide rim of his black hat, he looked like some hardened Clint Eastwood character. His eyes glittered in the low lighting, his mouth a thin line of indifference.

And yet he took her breath away. Every strong, familiar inch of him.

She dragged her gaze away, staring intently at the colorful label that circled the brown glass bottle in her hand until her pulse slowed to an almost human rate of speed instead of that of a hummingbird.

Even in a rowdy, crowded bar, surrounded by strangers and the teeth-rattling thrum of a noisy band, she was still unaccountably attracted to him. He hadn't touched her intimately since that night in the barn two weeks ago, yet she still felt the whisper of his hands and mouth on her naked flesh.

She shivered at the memory and took a long swallow of her light beer to extinguish the fire sparking to life low in her belly.

When Mitch's hand closed on her arm, she jumped.

"Sorry, didn't mean to startle you."

He was talking at a near-normal volume now, and she realized the band had slipped into a much slower song.

"Let's dance," he said. Then, without waiting for a reply, he slid off his stool and pulled her down to the floor beside him.

Fingers linked together, he led her to the dance floor, then swung her around and into his arms.

He held her entirely too close...not too close for society's standards, especially in this place, but too close for her peace of mind. For her body to maintain its natural calm.

One of his hands clutched hers. The other rested at the small of her back, his arm wrapped around her waist. His tall form brushed against her in all the right spots—chest to breasts, stomach to stomach, pelvis to pelvis. Everywhere they touched, rockets went off beneath her skin.

If he hadn't been holding her up, she thought she probably would have melted to the floor. As it was, her feet felt like they were barely touching the ground.

The music flowed all around them, and for the moment she let herself pretend this was more than their first date, more than two old friends who were toying with the idea of getting more seriously involved.

She imagined they were old lovers, maybe even a married couple, still very much in love. Out on the town for their anniversary, or perhaps just for an evening away from the kids.

The hand on her back shifted slightly lower, caressing the upper curve of her buttock and drawing her snug against his arousal.

It stunned her still that he was so obviously attracted to her. After all the years she'd pined for him from afar, to suddenly have him notice her as a woman and show sexual interest left her feeling confused and off-balance. Especially when he could make love to her with abandon one minute, then leave her hanging for two full weeks without so much as a phone call.

But he was trying. His suggestion that they try dating might not have been the smoothest invitation she'd ever received, and this might not be the greatest first date she'd ever gone on, but she gave him an A for effort.

And an A-plus for the way he made her heart beat faster, her knees turn to jelly, and her insides feel like she was riding up and down in an elevator car.

She sighed and closed her eyes, forgetting that they were in the middle of a crowded dance floor. As far as she was concerned, there was only Mitch and herself and the electricity arcing between them.

His rough jaw scraped her cheek as he leaned in close, his warm breath stirring her hair as he leaned in to speak above her ear.

"Want to get out of here?"

She blinked, raising her head to meet his gaze. His gray eyes burned with barely banked desire, and it was all she could do to remain upright.

She didn't think, didn't weigh the pros and cons, she simply responded in the only way her heart and body would allow. "Yes."

Four

Even as he half-dragged Emma out of the Silver Spur and across the gravel parking lot, Mitch called himself seven kinds of fool.

He'd purposely brought her here, knowing the bar would be noisy and crowded. Knowing there would be no chance of him being overcome by lust and making a move on her.

Ha! So much for that theory. His brilliant plan had backfired almost at the speed of light.

It had started innocently enough. Sit at the bar, sip a beer. The decibel level of the music and surrounding conversations made small talk impossible, which he considered a good thing.

But then he'd gone and asked her to dance. What a colossal mistake.

What had he been thinking? If he was going to make such a blunder, he could have at least made the offer during a fast song or while people were two-stepping in a synchronized group.

But, no, he'd gone and asked her to dance to a slow song. One that required them to stand close, to touch just about everywhere.

And he'd willingly taken her into his arms, set them both to swaying. Only when he felt her breasts with their semi-erect peaks brushing against his chest had he realized he was in trouble.

But by then, it had been too late. The scent of her freshly washed hair and spicy floral perfume had invaded his nostrils. The brush of her hands and belly and hips had turned him hard in an instant.

And despite his best efforts to maintain control, to cool his jets and remind himself that he'd promised he wouldn't sleep with her again, he found himself leaning in and asking her to leave with him.

To hell with their drinks. To hell with his vow to keep things platonic. He wanted her...now, with a single-minded determination that made him feel like a bull charging a red flag.

Their feet crunched on the gravel of the parking lot as he led her to the pickup and lifted her inside. Slamming the door, he stalked around the front of the truck and climbed behind the wheel.

Before the sound of his door closing had finished echoing through the cab, he was on her. Reaching out, dragging her across the vinyl seat and kissing her senseless. His hands were everywhere, groping, yanking, tearing her clothes away so he could get to her naked flesh.

She tasted of the beer she'd drunk earlier but also like Emma. Sweet, womanly, innocent.

Her lips met his, matched him move for move as though

she could read his mind. Her tongue teased and tangled, parried when he thrust and thrust when he parried.

And her hands…her hands were at the buttons of his shirt, the belt at his waist, every bit as eager to strip him bare as he was to do the same to her.

Her willingness, her eagerness drove him, let him know he wasn't the only one raging with passion, scrambling to get closer, faster, now, now.

He let her push the shirt off his shoulders and fumble with his heavy busting bronco belt buckle while he yanked her denim skirt up around her hips. He whispered a prayer of thanks when he discovered only a pair of sheer panties, with no stockings to bar his way, and wasted no time shucking them down her slim legs.

She had his belt undone by then and was working on the button and zipper of his jeans. He released her long enough to cover her hands and help her along.

As soon as he was free, hard and aching, he stopped, took a deep breath, lifted his head and looked into her eyes. She was staring back, chest heaving, her expression one of impatience and longing.

He felt like he should say something…compliment her, tell her she was beautiful or he cared about her. But he couldn't think of a damn thing that wouldn't sound fake or forced, and his mouth was full of cotton, anyway.

So he scrapped the idea of trying to be romantic or chivalrous and simply leaned in to take her lips. She kissed him back, wrapping her arms around his neck and weaving her fingers through his hair.

Keeping his mouth firmly on hers, he laid her back along the seat of the cab and knelt between her legs. A small shift of her skirt and his pants, and he was inside her.

She was gloriously tight and wet and felt like heaven.

He let out a groan of pleasure, resting his brow against hers for a moment until his breathing and heartbeat returned to normal. Well, as normal as they were likely to get when he was this close to Emma, this close to pure bliss.

"You okay?" he asked, his voice strained. He sensed rather than saw her nod and felt her slick inner muscles tighten around him in assent.

It was all he could do not to moan in sweet agony.

She was amazing. Open and eager. Fluid and graceful, but at the same time wild and uninhibited.

Holding her was like holding a live wire. And that charge, that jolt of high-voltage electricity, rocked him to his core.

He'd been celibate ever since he found out Suzanne was cheating on him, so it was no small wonder he was ravenous for a woman's touch. It had almost been easier to simply grit his teeth and white-knuckle his way through the lack of sex in his life.

But now that he'd been with Emma, had had a woman's silky skin beneath his hands and feminine body enveloping his, he couldn't seem to get enough. He wanted her naked and writhing for him twenty-four hours a day.

One would think that for a man who'd been without a woman's company as long as he had, any woman would do. But something told him that wasn't quite true. Some part of him knew that if his dry spell hadn't been broken by Emma…it might not have been broken at all.

In all the time he'd been divorced from Suzanne, no one had even tempted him to break his celibacy.

No one until Emma, up in that loft.

And now here she was again, letting him take her. In the cab of his truck, no less.

If he were any kind of man, he would stop what he was

doing and let her up. Apologize and take her home. Or at the very least, take her somewhere decent to finish what they'd started—his place or a motel. Somewhere with a bed and clean sheets.

But he was too far gone, and he obviously wasn't that noble because instead of pulling away, he tugged her legs more snugly around his hips and pressed forward until he was as deep inside her as he could go.

Emma couldn't think, could barely breathe with Mitch's weight on top of her. His heat, his intensity, the feel of him filling her to overflowing.

She wanted him to move, to give her what she needed before the urge to scream became unbearable.

"Mitch, please," she whimpered, tightening her hold around his hips and neck.

Ripples of pleasure coursed through her and she gave a sigh of relief when he began to rock, thrusting into her with power and purpose. He wasted no time with added foreplay or spare caresses, and she didn't need them. All she wanted was him—hard, fast, now.

He sped up, driving into her with increasing force until her vision turned blurry around the edges and bursts of color went off behind her eyes and in her bloodstream. She bit her lip to keep from crying out…then cried out anyway when her orgasm broke and washed over her in a giant wave of sensation.

Mitch thrust once, twice more, before giving a shout of completion and stiffening above her. His breath panted in her ear, his heart pounding against her chest.

Long minutes passed before feeling returned to their limbs and they were able to move. Mitch hoisted himself off of her with a reluctant groan, then helped her sit up and rearrange her clothes. Once everything was back in order, they sat on opposite ends of the wide bench seat, staring straight ahead.

After a moment of awkward silence, she said, "Boy, we really fogged it up in here, didn't we?"

The windshield and side windows were smoky with condensation, blocking their view.

A beat passed, and then he let out a rough laugh. "Yeah, we sure did."

He leaned over to retrieve his Stetson from her side of the cab's floor, where it had fallen during their wild groping, dusted it off and jammed it back on his head.

"You hungry?" he asked, fingers flexing on the steering wheel.

Now that both her nerves about their first date and the intense passion of their quick joining had passed, she realized she was starving.

"Definitely."

Brushing his shirt sleeve across the glass so he could see, he started the engine and pulled slowly out of the parking lot. Ten minutes later, they were back in one of the red vinyl booths of Rosie's Café.

The diner was open till ten, but evening wasn't a busy time, so only one waitress and one cook were working, and Mitch and Emma were the only customers. They sat on opposite sides of a booth near the rear of the restaurant and ordered glasses of iced tea and two plates of the special— spaghetti and meat sauce, with garlic bread on the side.

Normally, Emma would have avoided any type of garlic, onions and the like on a date, but since Mitch was having some, too, and they'd already gotten all the hot and heavy business out of their systems before dinner, she thought she was probably safe.

They made small talk while they wound pasta around

their forks and sopped up red sauce with the chunks of garlic bread.

"So, how's your family?" she wanted to know.

"Good. Mom and Dad keep themselves busy with the ranch, and I help out when I can."

"And Chase?"

Chase was younger by four years but every inch as handsome and charming. Even though he'd grown up on a horse and cattle ranch and knew the workings of one as well as she and Mitch, his interests had always lain elsewhere. Instead of working the land, he found greater pleasure in the business world, buying up struggling companies to either help them revamp and have a second shot at success or breaking them up to sell off for profit. From what she'd heard, he was doing quite well for himself.

"He's fine. You know Chase, he's off working on some kind of deal again. Last I heard, he was in Chicago, but we expect him back soon."

She nodded and wiped the corners of her mouth with her napkin before taking a sip of tea.

"You know, what happened tonight...I didn't plan it that way."

He kept his eyes glued to his plate, so she had no doubt what part of the evening he was referring to.

"I told myself I wouldn't touch you, no matter what. We were just supposed to go out and have fun."

She let a moment pass, deciding how best to respond. Finally, she said, "I had fun," before taking another bite of tender spaghetti.

She had the pleasure of watching his eyes widen and his mouth drop open slightly. But only for a second. In the blink of an eye, he caught himself and once again schooled his features into a mask of stern control.

Honestly, he was the most rigid man she'd ever met.

He'd always been serious but not *this* serious. She blamed Suzanne for the change, and it wasn't a positive one.

Which was why it was almost amusing to do or say things that knocked him off balance and broke through that steely exterior. Lord knew someone needed to.

"Relax, Mitch," she said on half a laugh. "For heaven's sake, you're acting like you personally escorted me to the lion's den. It was sex. Incredibly good, incredibly hot sex. But I wish you'd stop apologizing…. You're starting to give me a complex."

He studied her from across the booth, and she could see the wheels turning in his mind.

"What do you suggest we do?" he asked in a low voice. "Continue having incredibly good, incredibly hot sex every chance we get?"

At his words, a bolt of heat lightning shot straight to her feminine core. "Yes." *God, yes. Please.*

This time, he didn't bother trying to control his reaction as he goggled at her.

"Are you crazy?" he hissed. "How can you be so cavalier about this?"

"How can you be so uptight about it? We're hardly strangers; we've known each other since we were kids. If any two people should be comfortable around each other in just about any situation, it's us."

She waved her fork at him while she chewed. "And I don't know about you, but I'm enjoying myself. The sex is great, very satisfying, and I like being with you. We haven't spent this much time together since before you married Suzanne."

As soon as the name passed her lips, Emma wished she could take it back. His mouth flattened into a thin line and his eyes turned dark. Just as they always did at the mention of his ex-wife.

"Sorry," she mumbled, letting her gaze skitter away.

After playing with her food for a minute or two, she took a deep breath and lifted her head, determined to look him straight in the eye.

"All I'm saying is that I've missed hanging out with you. And if I'd known the sex was going to be so good, I'd have probably seduced you way back in high school."

At that, one dark eyebrow winged upward. "You would have, huh?"

"Oh, yeah," she said with a nod. "Either you or Chase. I figure since you're so alike in other ways, you're probably equally talented in bed."

That brought a deep scowl to his face, and she nearly chuckled.

Note to self. Don't tell the man you're sleeping with that you can find another man who can satisfy you just as well as he does. Especially if the two are related.

"Look," she said when he remained stoically silent for so long, she feared smoke would seep out of his ears. "You're the one who said we should go out for a while, see where things lead. So why can't we keep doing that?"

"Because every time we go out," he told her through clenched teeth, "we end up rolling around like…like… monkeys in heat."

Monkeys? In heat? She wasn't sure she appreciated that particular imagery.

"Most men would be thrilled to have all of their dates end with them getting lucky."

"Is that so?" His eyes glittered, but she couldn't tell if it was with amusement or warning. "I guess I'm not like most men, then."

Well, that was certainly true. For better or worse, Mitch was unlike any man she'd ever known before.

With her heart pounding in her chest, she licked her lips nervously and asked, "Does that mean you don't want to sleep with me anymore?"

A muscle in his jaw jumped as he contemplated his answer. "I didn't say that," he replied finally, sounding reluctant.

Emma hoped her face didn't show her intense relief, but it washed over her all the same, causing her stomach to flutter.

"Do you not want to go out anymore at all?"

"I didn't say that, either."

"Then may I make a suggestion?"

She was loathe to press her luck, to push him into a corner or evoke a response from him that she might not care for quite as much as the ones she'd gotten so far. But she also didn't want to continue having this conversation with him or know that every time they were together, he'd suffer a bout of postcoital guilt.

"What's that?" he asked.

"Let's go back to your original plan. We go out, we enjoy ourselves. If we feel like having sex, we can, but without any pressure *or guilt*," she stressed, "on either side. And we'll see where it takes us, just like you suggested."

His eyebrows drew together and lines formed around his frowning mouth. "Throwing my own words back at me, huh? Guess I should be more careful of what I say around you."

She smiled, reassured by his comment that he wasn't going to cut her loose and demand they go back to being just friends and neighbors.

"Guess you should."

His lips curved up on one side and he pushed his empty plate aside, folding his arms in front of him on the tabletop. "So, what do you want to do on our next date?"

"Maybe a movie," she offered. And then, with a straight face, she added, "Followed by hot, sweaty, monkey sex."

This time, her mention of sex didn't set his eyes or jaw to twitching. Instead, he met her gaze and said, "How does Saturday sound? I'll pick you up at eight."

Five

Mitch pushed his plate away and released a breath that only seemed to tighten the waistband of his pants. Once again, he'd eaten too much. But it was Emma's fault for being such a damn fine cook.

They'd been following their dating plan for three weeks now, and this was the third time he'd had dinner at her place. It was becoming something of a weekly custom.

And though it had made him nervous at first to sit across the table from Wyatt, wondering if the man was going to jump up at any moment and threaten to castrate Mitch for taking advantage of his daughter, he had to admit he was starting to enjoy the evenings he spent in the Davis household.

Each meal Emma fixed tasted better than the last. He didn't miss the fact, either, that she made a point of preparing his favorite dishes on the nights he came over, like meatloaf and pork chops. And she always had homemade biscuits, fresh out of the oven, ever since his first visit when he'd eaten six and told her how good they were.

"Would you like any more?" Emma asked before pushing back her chair and collecting the bowls of mashed potatoes and green beans.

"No, thank you. I couldn't eat another bite." He patted his belly and slumped in his chair with an appreciative smile on his face.

"My girl sure can cook, can't she?" Wyatt asked, beaming proudly. "She takes after her mother."

"Yes, sir," Mitch agreed. "I can't remember the last time I tasted such good food."

His dinners these days pretty much consisted of single-serving microwave meals or leftovers his mother sent over when she got worried he wasn't eating right.

"Don't tell my mother I said that, though," he added.

Wyatt chuckled. "Don't worry, your secret's safe with me."

Then he turned to Emma, who was busy transferring the remainder of the meal into smaller containers and slipping them in the fridge.

"If you don't need any help, honey, do you mind if Mitch and I step outside for a few minutes?"

Mitch was a little surprised by the request, but judging by the friendly expression on the older man's face, he didn't think Emma's father planned to take him out to the barn and shoot him. At least he hoped not.

"No, I'm fine," she told them, piling dishes into the sink and running hot water over them. "You two go ahead. But no smoking, all right?" She shot her father a warning look. "I mean it, Pop. Mitch, don't let him light one of those filthy cigars."

Wyatt winked at Mitch, his blue eyes twinkling as he

pushed to his feet. "A man can't have any fun around here," he pretended to grumble.

Mitch didn't know that he would agree with that statement. Considering the number of times in the past few weeks that he and Emma had sneaked out to the barn or up to her room when her father wasn't around, he could reliably say a man could have a great deal of fun around this place.

But he didn't think it would be very smart to point that out to Wyatt. Not when he was doing his damnedest *not* to let the man know he was sleeping with his daughter.

Emma, up to her elbows now in sudsy water, shook her head but chose not to respond to her father's complaint.

The legs of Mitch's chair scraped the floor as he got up and followed Wyatt onto the front porch. The older man took a seat on the solid wooden swing to one side of the kitchen door and pulled a plump brown stogie from his front shirt pocket. He ran the cigar under his nose, inhaling deeply, then tucked it away again with a sigh of regret.

"A couple of puffs after dinner, that's my limit. But she worries about me, so most of the time all I get to do is sniff the damn thing."

Moving to a spot in front of Wyatt, Mitch leaned back against the porch railing, feet crossed at the ankle, hands resting on either side of his hips.

After several more minutes passed in silence, he said, "You wanted to talk to me, sir?"

"Yes. Yes, I did."

Wyatt slapped his hands down on his knees and rose to his feet, coming to stand beside Mitch, facing the other direction.

"Emma is my pride and joy, you know that."

"Yes, sir."

"And I worry about her, just as much as she worries about me."

"Yes, sir," Mitch murmured again, not sure where this conversation was headed.

"I worry especially about what will happen with her after I'm gone."

It took a moment for that to sink in, and when it did, Mitch's gut clenched. "Is something wrong, Mr. Davis? Are you sick?" He couldn't quite bring himself to ask if the man was dying, but that was the message flashing across the front of his brain.

"Hell, no," Wyatt denied firmly. "Healthy as an ox, according to the doctor. But I'm not getting any younger, and accidents happen. There's no telling how long any of us will get to be on this earth. And when my time comes, I'd like to know my girl is taken care of."

Mitch's breathing had returned to normal, but his heart was still beating just a little faster than it should. "I can understand that."

"That's where you come in."

One eyebrow lifted in curiosity. "Excuse me?"

"I've got a proposition for you, my boy." Wyatt twisted to face him more fully and slapped him on the arm. "Emma's an only child, and as sexist as it might sound, I don't have any sons to deed this land to when I die. My girl loves this place and is great at helping me out with the business end of things, but she won't want to run the ranch after I'm gone."

Mitch made a noncommittal noise, still not sure what Wyatt was getting at.

"Our families have always been close, you and Emma grew up together, and your land borders ours. So I'll come right out and say what I'm thinking, Mitch. I'd like you to marry my daughter."

He blinked, stunned into speechlessness. Where his

heart had been running a bit too fast only minutes before, it now seemed to slow almost to a stop.

"I know, I know," Emma's father continued. "It's an odd request. Not to mention extremely meddling of me. But I've watched the two of you together these past weeks. Emma's happy, and it does my heart good to see the two of you getting so serious.

"I don't mind telling you that your parents and I have always sort of hoped our two families would end up connecting this way. We never wanted to pressure you kids in any way, but there were many nights that we discussed the possibilities over a couple hands of cards."

That was news to Mitch. As close as their families had been and as much time as he and Chase had spent with Emma growing up, it had honestly never occurred to him that either he or his brother might wind up interested in Emma romantically.

Not that there was anything wrong with her. On the contrary, she had always been a nice, good-looking girl. But she'd practically been their sister.

He wondered if Chase had ever thought of her in any other way and made a mental note to ask the next time he saw his brother.

"I know it's a strange thing to ask, and you'll want to think it over. But I'd feel more comfortable leaving the Double D to you, as my son-in-law, knowing you'll keep it in good shape. Emma would do her best, but she'd have to hire on a lot more help, and I'm just not sure her heart would be in it.

"You're a responsible man. Decent and trustworthy. If you married my Emma and took over the running of this ranch, I'd know Emma was being taken care of."

Mitch rubbed his jaw, briefly entertaining the notion that

he was hallucinating. It just didn't make sense that in this day and age, a father was standing beside him, trying to work out the details of an arranged marriage for his daughter.

And yet, he understood Wyatt's motivation, the love and concern behind the offer. The Double D had been in Wyatt's family for generations. Wyatt had lived here all his life, loving and working the ranch. He'd grown up, married, and raised a family all in the same house, on the same land.

Mitch understood the man's desire to make sure the ranch was taken care of after he was gone. To see that his *daughter* was well taken care of, as well.

It might sound callous or overly chauvinistic to some, but Wyatt only wanted the best for Emma and his homestead.

Not that Mitch was honestly considering saying yes. When his marriage to Suzanne had ended, he'd sworn never to get lured into that trap again. He and Emma might have been heating up the sheets these past few weeks, but being good together in bed didn't mean they had to get leg-shackled.

"I'm sorry, Mr. Davis," he said, returning his hands to the porch railing, "but I don't think—"

"Now, now," Wyatt interrupted. "Don't answer just yet. Take some time, give it some serious thought. I understand the significance of my proposition and don't want you agreeing to anything you aren't absolutely sure about. Emma deserves better than that, and so do you."

The older man slapped him on the back and took a few steps away, heading toward the kitchen door. "But just so you know, I'd consider it a personal favor if you and Emma got hitched. I can't think of anyone I'd rather have running this place and looking after my girl after I'm gone."

Shaking his head in puzzlement, Mitch pushed off of the railing and followed Wyatt back to the house.

The arresting aroma of fresh-brewed coffee hit him the

minute he stepped into the kitchen. Emma had set a platter of homemade cookies in the center of the table and was pouring coffee for the three of them.

As they returned to their chairs, she slid a mug toward him and his heart lurched to realize how much care she'd taken with everything. The meal, the hominess of the room they were sitting in, the cookies on the table, and each cup of coffee doctored just as the drinker liked it.

As wives went, he could do a lot worse than Emma, that was for sure. She was kind and considerate, a terrific cook and sexy as all get out.

He didn't imagine everyone would think so. She didn't possess the fantasy hourglass figure, and what she did have, she tended to hide beneath blue jeans and button-down blouses.

But she wore those jeans like no one he'd ever see before. She didn't pour herself into them the way Suzanne had, but they weren't loose and baggy, either. They fit just right—snug where a man could appreciate it most and roomy enough in other places to plague his imagination.

And since he'd seen her naked, *felt* her naked beneath him on many recent occasions, he happened to know that her less than fashionably ideal form was actually quite perfect.

Her breasts were pert and pretty and just large enough to fit his hands. Her waist was slim, tapering down to narrow hips that made his mouth water. And her legs were as long and muscular as a colt's.

He'd come up with that particular analogy the last time she'd sat astride him and ridden him into a foaming lather.

The memory sent blood shooting to all the wrong places—at least while he was sitting across the table from her father—and he immediately tried to redirect his wayward thoughts. Wyatt's invitation to marry her and take over his land pretty much did the trick.

The only problem was, this time, the idea didn't seem quite so repugnant.

As he sipped his coffee and listened with half an ear to what Emma and Wyatt were saying, he pictured himself standing in front of a preacher again, speaking those holy vows that had backfired on him once. A skitter of icy fear snaked down his spine.

But then he imagined being married to Emma. She wouldn't be like Suzanne, that was for sure. She was the homey type and would take great pride in taking care of him and their household. He would have piping-hot meals to look forward to on a daily basis, and even hotter nights spent in her arms. She would laugh and maybe even make him smile in return.

That was certainly something he could get used to. And he knew that he could be married to Emma, be a good husband, without getting too emotionally attached to her.

Men were blessed that way. He'd married once for love and been kicked in the crotch for his trouble. No way was he interested in a repeat performance. But he could live with her, sleep with her and make her happy without risking his heart.

His only concern was that Emma might not. Women were different, and she was perhaps more sensitive than most. What if she developed feelings for him that he couldn't reciprocate? What if she read too much into their arrangement and ended up getting hurt?

But she seemed to understand that he was once bitten, twice shy. In all the time they'd been dating and sleeping together, she'd never once asked more of him than he was willing to give. She didn't bring up Suzanne or ask him to pour out his soul so she could analyze his feelings and try to fix them. She simply accepted their relationship—and him—for what it was.

If she could handle a marriage to him in the same way, then they might just have a shot at building some sort of life together and fulfilling her father's wishes, as well.

And it was no small consideration that if he took Wyatt up on his offer, his own parents would stop pressuring him to get over his ex's betrayal, get on with his life, and find a better woman to settle down with.

Emma's and Wyatt's voices buzzed in his ears, his thoughts seeming to race faster than his brain could process them. What he was contemplating made his temperature rise at the same time a cold sweat began to trickle between his shoulder blades.

Suddenly, he realized his companions had stopped talking. The room was eerily silent, and, when he raised his head, he found two nearly identical sets of eyes gazing back at him.

"Sorry," he said, feeling like an idiot. "Guess my mind wandered."

"That's all right," Emma replied softly, gifting him with a comforting smile. "Pop was just fishing for compliments on my behalf, anyway."

Still smiling, she floated up from her chair and made her way to the sink to rinse her coffee cup. He watched her cross the room, mesmerized by the fluid grace of her movements, by her long, slim limbs and tight, round bottom.

His gut tightened and a sensation like warm melted butter crawled through his veins.

Before he could talk himself out of it, he pushed his chair back and got to his feet. "Care to take a walk with me, Emma?"

Her head whipped around, startlement in her clear blue eyes. She reached over to turn off the water, then dried her hands on a nearby dish towel before turning to fully face him.

"Um…okay." Her gaze skittered to her father for a brief second. "You don't mind if we leave you alone for a while, do you, Pop?"

"'Course not," he answered quickly, waving them away. "You two go on. There's plenty around here to keep me busy."

Mitch opened the front door and held it while Emma passed through. He waited until she'd crossed the width of the porch and stepped down into the yard before tipping his head back in Wyatt's direction.

"I thought about it," he said in a low voice, not wanting Emma to overhear, "and I've decided to take you up on your offer."

He stepped outside, closing the door behind him, but not before he caught the grin of pure delight on Wyatt Davis's bearded face.

Emma turned in time to see Mitch come down off the porch steps and catch up with her. Without speaking, he took her hand and started walking.

They moved away from the pale streaks of yellow light shining through the windows of the house, but the moon overhead shone brightly enough to illuminate their path.

"Where are we going?" she finally broke the silence to ask.

"Nowhere special. I just thought we'd find some place private to talk."

"Just talk?" she shot back with a teasing grin. From her experience, he was fine with talking in public. It was other things he preferred to do in private.

"Just talk."

His tone was so serious, so unyielding, a ripple of fear caused her stomach to tighten.

This was it, she thought. He was getting ready to break up with her.

She shouldn't be surprised. She'd known it was coming—eventually.

But that didn't keep her heart from twisting, didn't keep regret from tensing her muscles and slowing her step.

Just a little longer. That's all she'd wanted—just a little longer to be with him, to love him, to pretend he loved her, too.

A few more days, a few more weeks…then she'd have been able to let him go. She might even have been the one to end it before he had a chance.

Breathing deeply, she tried to remain calm, tried to tell herself it was inevitable and probably for the best. She was a big girl, she could handle it.

She would miss being with him, but they could still be friends. Instead of going out as a couple, they would run into each other on the street and make small talk. Instead of making love, they would smile and pretend they'd never seen each other naked, never made each other pant and scream in ecstasy.

Piece of cake.

And maybe next she'd attempt to leap tall buildings in a single bound.

When she felt a tug on her arm, she realized Mitch had stopped walking. Looking around, she decided they must be out behind the house. She hadn't been paying enough attention to know how far.

"So…what did you want to talk about?" she prompted, even though she knew perfectly well. She swallowed hard and blinked, telling herself not to cry.

He leaned back against the bark of a tall catalpa tree and took her other hand, pulling her close. Their bodies brushed and she reveled in his warmth, even as she wondered why he was bothering when he just planned to dump her, anyway.

"Our future," he said.

Here it came. By *our future*, he meant the lack thereof.

Her heart was racing, her palms turning damp with nervousness. And she knew that when she spoke, her voice would quaver. "What about our future?"

"I've been thinking."

Of course he had, and he'd decided he'd had enough of her.

"These past few weeks…we've had fun. We've been pretty good together."

Yes, they had been. More than good. At times, they'd been phenomenal. But apparently that didn't matter to him.

"And I've been thinking…"

Yes, yes, he'd said that already.

"That maybe we should make it permanent."

Of course. Ever since Suzanne had left him—

She stopped. Stopped thinking, stopped blinking, stopped breathing. Had he just said…?

What had he just said?

"Excuse me?" she practically wheezed with what little air was left in her lungs.

"Emma," he said slowly, his eyes dark and solemn as he stared into her own. "Will you marry me?"

Six

Emma had heard of being struck speechless before, but she'd never actually experienced it until this moment. Her head was spinning so fast, she feared she might pass out, and, even though her lungs burned for air, she couldn't seem to inhale.

He'd just asked her to marry him. Mitch. Had asked *her*. To marry *him*. When she'd thought for sure he was about to dump her instead and had been bracing herself for the worst.

Finally she managed to suck in a long, much-needed breath. "But—"

"It may not be a love match," he said, running his hands up her arms to cup her shoulders and essentially cutting off whatever she'd been about to say. "I know that, but we get along well enough to make a marriage work. I like you, you like me. There's no doubt we're good in bed. And I'll take care of you, no matter what. You can trust me on that."

In the space of a heartbeat, she went from being elated

that he might have feelings for her after all…enough to propose to her…to being crushed by his blatant admission that he didn't love her at all but merely saw a marriage to her as something that would be convenient and comfortable for both of them.

Her first instinct was to tell him what he could do with his less-than-inspiring offer. But then she began to think of how much courage it had taken for him to even ask.

Suzanne had done a real number on him, and she knew exactly how bitter he still was over her betrayal. It was a huge step for him to come to her now and ask her to marry him…even if it wasn't her idea of a dream proposal.

And she *had* been in love with him for as long as she could remember. This was her chance to be with him, regardless of the circumstances.

Maybe he didn't love her. Maybe he never would. Or maybe he just didn't love her *yet*. People changed. And people most especially healed after painful breakups.

If she married him, then every day would be another chance for her to erase a little more of Suzanne from his mind and heart and instill herself there instead. Not all women were like his scheming, two-timing ex, and all she needed was an opportunity to prove that to him.

A small voice inside her head warned her not to get her hopes up. That a woman couldn't change a man, and there was no use trying.

But Emma didn't want to change Mitch. She liked him just the way he was…or she had before he'd married up with that tramp.

And now, she simply wanted to be around when his battered heart finally healed and he got over his ex. For that, she could put a couple of years into a marriage that lacked the emotions she so dearly craved.

As long as she believed there was a chance he'd come around, a chance he could grow to love her as much as she already loved him.

A shiver of anticipation raced through her, settling low in her belly and spreading warmly outward.

She was doing the right thing. She knew she was.

Leaning close, she put her hands on either side of his waist and pressed her lips to the corner of his mouth. "Yes," she whispered. "Yes, I'll marry you."

His fingers tightened on her shoulders and she thought she felt him shudder against her.

"Good," he said with a matter-of-fact nod. He kicked himself away from the trunk of the tree and took her hand. "Let's go back to the house and tell your dad."

Her eyes widened in surprise and she let out a nervous chuckle. When he tugged at her arm, she tugged back.

"Wait a minute. Don't you want to celebrate?"

Since he was standing as still and immovable as a stone statue, she went to him, pressing herself along his tall frame and raising her face to his.

"Yeah, right. Celebrate." He bent in to kiss her, just a quick, hard peck on her lips, then he straightened again and dragged her after him.

She laughed, increasing her steps to keep up and thinking that from now on, her life—her life with Mitch—was going to be very interesting, indeed.

Emma took a sip of her wine—her second glass of the evening, and she'd only arrived an hour ago.

The Ramsey's sprawling one-story house was filled with guests, family and friends gathered by Mitch's mother to help celebrate their engagement. Flowers and balloons decorated the large, hardwood living room, and a banner that said Congratulations Mitch And Emma! hung over the stone fireplace.

It was all very thoughtful…and very intimidating.

But as soon as Theresa Ramsey had heard the news, she'd insisted she be allowed to throw a party for them, inviting half the town to what had transformed from wine, cheese and classical music to louder country tunes and free-flowing alcohol.

Ironically, it was his parents' enthusiasm about their engagement and all the plans his mother immediately began to launch that had seemed to turn Mitch off. From the time they'd announced their plans to marry—first to her father and then to his mom and dad—the same night he'd proposed, he'd seemed to shut down, showing no interest whatsoever in their engagement or upcoming nuptials.

He'd reluctantly agreed to his mother's arrangements and told Emma to do whatever she wanted as far as the wedding was concerned. He was leaving it up to her to set the date and decide on all of the preparations.

She understood him not wanting to get involved. How many men really wanted to play a part in deciding on flowers and color schemes and girlie things like that?

But she'd at least expected him to help her choose a place for the ceremony—the church or his parents' backyard?—and maybe offer suggestions for the guest list. Instead, he'd washed his hands of the entire situation, leaving her feeling very much alone.

They'd arrived tonight together, at his mother's prompting. Theresa had mapped things out so that everyone else arrived before the guests of honor, and when Mitch and Emma walked through the door, it was to mingled shouts of "Surprise!" and "Congratulations!"

She hadn't seen Mitch since.

Swallowing past the lump of emotion threatening to

clog her throat, Emma forced a smile to her lips for the gentleman who'd just told her a supposedly amusing story of which she hadn't heard a word.

It was Mitch's way, that's all, she told herself. He was a private person who didn't like crowds or parties and especially didn't like people making a fuss over him.

He'd also been married before. A marriage he'd been eager for and expected to last forever. Going through all of this again couldn't be easy for him.

He was probably being flooded by painful memories and might even be considering what all of these guests were thinking about his latest engagement. *Here he goes again. Maybe this time it will work out. Wonder if Emma will end up stepping out on him, too.*

Emma didn't believe any of their friends and neighbors would think such things about him, but she knew how Mitch's mind worked these days. He'd become incredibly sensitive and prickly since Suzanne's infidelity. As Emma imagined most men would.

But she would never hurt him that way and only needed a chance to prove it. She only needed time for him to begin to believe it.

That didn't mean she wasn't still nervous about the entire situation, however. Couples who were madly in love and one-hundred-percent dedicated to having a happy, healthy marriage suffered from butterflies and cold feet. Emma was positively petrified.

As much as she loved Mitch already, as much as she wanted to be his wife, having a fiancé who treated her coolly and was indifferent to their wedding plans was enough to bring doubts the size of Texas to the forefront of her mind.

The room around her felt suddenly too small, packed

with people to a claustrophobic degree. Her chest tightened and her breathing became slightly labored.

She needed some fresh air and just a few minutes alone to calm her nerves.

Keeping a smile on her face and nodding to acquaintances as she passed, she made her way into the kitchen and out a side door. The Ramsey home had a great wraparound porch that connected to three sides of the house, with three different entrances. The better to slip away without being seen than if she'd been forced to leave through the front door.

Once outside, she stepped to the railing, set her wineglass aside and took a deep breath as she stared across the darkening landscape. Nails digging into wood, she studied the colors streaking the horizon as dusk drifted into night.

The cool air felt nice on her heated skin, and she finally relaxed her grip on the railing enough to reach for her glass and take another small sip.

"Getting a little crowded in there, isn't it?"

Emma jumped at the sound of the deep male voice coming out of the darkness and turned to find Mitch's brother, Chase, standing just a few feet away. Her heart pounded as she watched him step out of the shadows.

He was dressed in jeans and cowboy boots like just about every other man in attendance but was also wearing a tan jacket over his blue chambray shirt. The highball glass in his right hand was half filled with amber liquid and three rapidly melting ice cubes.

"Chase," she said, still somewhat breathless from the shock of having him sneak up on her. "I didn't know you were here. Mitch told me you were in Chicago or some such place on business."

"I was. But I couldn't miss my brother's engagement party to my favorite neighbor." He smiled gently and leaned in to kiss her cheek. "How are you, Emma?"

"Fine," she replied letting her gaze slide away from his. "How are you?"

"That's funny," he said, taking a sip of his drink and completely ignoring her polite question. "For someone who's supposed to be celebrating her upcoming marriage, I'd expect you to be a little more than just 'fine.' In fact, I'd expect you to be fairly vibrating with excitement."

"I'm excited," she told him, eyes still riveted to the porch floor. Her response sounded lame even to her own ears.

He gave a short huff of amusement. "If this is excited, I'd hate to see you depressed. Come on," he said softly, reaching out to knuckle her chin up and force her gaze to his. "You can't fool me, Emma. We've known each other too long. What's wrong?"

"Nothing," she tried to assure him with an overly bright grin, even as tears prickled behind her eyes.

"Emma…"

His tone was so soft, the look he gave her so sympathetic that she buried her face in the soft fabric of his suit jacket and burst into tears.

For several long minutes, he simply held her and let her cry, patting her back and murmuring nonsensical words of comfort. When she finally got hold of her emotions and lifted her head, he handed her a handkerchief to wipe her eyes and nose.

"Thank you," she said with a sniff, knowing she would have to slink back inside to fix her makeup and make sure her eyes weren't all red and puffy before anyone else got a look at her.

"Now are you ready to tell me what the problem is?"

She shook her head. "I shouldn't. You're his brother, and I'm sure I'm just overly nervous and emotional about the wedding."

"But…" he prompted. "My brother has obviously done something typically stupid or insensitive."

"That's just it," she said quietly, glancing at the handkerchief she was worrying with her fingertips. If it had been made of tissue rather than a sturdy cotton weave, she'd have shredded it into a million pieces by now. "He hasn't done anything. Ever since he proposed, he's been acting like he doesn't even *want* to get married. He hasn't shown a single bit of interest in the wedding plans or our future or even this party that your mother is so excited about and put so much time and energy into."

She waved a hand toward the crowded house, then dabbed once again at her flooding eyes. "I thought that being engaged to Mitch, being married to him, would make me happy, but now I wish we'd stuck to just sleeping together."

Chase's eyes widened at that declaration, but she ignored it. Obviously, Mitch wasn't the only person in town who expected her to be an innocent virgin until her dying—or wedding, as the case may be—day.

"Look," Chase said, rubbing her arms, left bare by her sleeveless dress, in a comforting gesture. "The reason for all of this is simple. My brother is an ass. His first mistake was hooking up with Suzanne, which anyone who was paying attention could have told him was a situation that had *disaster* written all over it. His second mistake was wasting so much as a minute being sorry when she left. And his third mistake…"

He paused to brush a lock of hair behind her ear and

offer a gentle smile. "His third and by far largest mistake, was making you cry when he should be holding on to you with both hands and letting you know every minute how much you mean to him."

At that, Emma's lungs hitched and tears started rolling down her face again.

Chase pulled her into his arms and patted her back. "*Shh.* He doesn't mean to hurt your feelings, he's just a little mixed up right now. You know what a number Suzanne's infidelity did on him. He doesn't know what he wants anymore."

She understood what he was saying, but it didn't make her feel any better. She was still in the distressing predicament of being engaged to a man she wasn't at all sure wanted to be with her.

Behind her, she heard the side door of the house open and footsteps echo on the wooden planks of the porch floor. Pushing away from Chase's embrace, she wiped her nose and cheeks, embarrassed to have been caught crying at her own engagement party.

When she turned, it wasn't a random guest standing a few feet away, but Mitch, who was glaring at her with dark, angry eyes.

"Well," he drawled, his voice as sharp as a knife edge, "I guess it's a good thing I found out about this before the wedding rather than after. It would be pretty stupid of me to marry *another* liar and cheater."

She felt Chase tense behind her a second before he growled, "Now, wait just a damn minute—"

"And with my own brother." Mitch stared past her, a sneer twisting his mouth.

"Mitch…" she said quickly, hoping to diffuse the situation before it got any worse "…it's not what you think."

Taking a step forward, she stretched a hand toward his chest only to drop it when he moved back and gave her a look that could have cut through glass.

"It never is, is it?" he replied nastily.

"Watch it, Mitch," Chase murmured from behind her in a threatening tone. "I'm not above bloodying your nose at your own engagement party."

Mitch took a menacing step forward, his furious gaze locked on his brother, completely ignoring Emma, who stood between them. "You're not above making time with my fiancé, either, are you?"

"Enough," she snapped, turning sideways and holding her arms out to stop both men in their tracks. "That's enough. Chase, I appreciate your help, but I think Mitch and I need a few minutes alone."

Chase relaxed his stance enough to meet her eyes. "You sure?"

"I'm sure."

"All right, but I'll be just inside. Yell if you need me."

She nodded but kept her mouth shut, knowing that if she said anything, Mitch would take it as a further sign that she was siding—not to mention cheating—with his brother.

Chase moved around them to the door, keeping a wary eye on his brother the entire time. With his hand on the knob, he said, "Hurt her and I'll make you sorry," before returning to the crowded house.

"Too late," Mitch muttered, even though his brother was no longer there to hear him. "I'm already sorry."

Her heart squeezed at his implication, but she lifted her chin and forced herself to face him head-on.

"Mitch, what you saw… Chase was only comforting me because I was upset. We weren't involved in some clandestine meeting. I'm not Suzanne," she added with feeling. "I would never betray you like that, and neither would your brother."

His eyes narrowed, jaw tightening, and he lifted his hands to his hips. "I know what I saw."

"You saw me crying on your brother's shoulder, that's all."

But even as she said the words, she knew they were falling on deaf ears. No matter what she said, he wasn't going to believe her. He thought the worst because he'd been cheated on before and was still raw and aching from the experience. She could talk herself blue…for heaven's sake, she could show him photographs *proving* her faithfulness and he still wouldn't believe her.

A stab of regret pierced her belly and her heart began to ache as she realized this would never work. She couldn't marry Mitch. Couldn't maintain a relationship with him when it was obvious he would never trust her.

His reaction to her innocent conversation with his brother was enough to convince her of that. And she didn't want to be with someone who was automatically going to think the worst of her in every situation.

She couldn't live like that, always being watched, always being suspected and accused.

Taking a deep breath, she closed her eyes and prayed she wouldn't break down in front of him the way she had with Chase.

"You know, I don't think this is going to work," she told him, glad when her voice came out solid and self-assured, because her insides were shaking like the San Andreas Fault. "There's nothing going on between Chase and me. That's the God's honest truth. But you'll never believe it, never believe a word I say because you're still not over Suzanne. And I can't marry a man who doesn't trust me."

She opened and closed her hands at her sides, not

knowing what else to do with them and half-afraid she would reach for him, effectively ruining any resolve she had about calling things off.

"I'm sorry, but I think it would be better if we called off the wedding."

For several long seconds, Mitch stared at her, gaze intense, a muscle jumping in his clenched jaw. "You're right. Things never would have worked out."

Turning on his heel, he stepped off the porch and disappeared into the night. Emma watched him go, knowing she'd made the right decision but hating it all the same.

Mitch was the one man she'd always loved. And now, she realized, he was also the one man she could never have.

Seven

Emma pushed herself up from the bathroom floor, using the edge of the tub as leverage. Still shaky and weak, she made her way to the sink to rinse her mouth and splash a bit of cool water on her face.

This was the fourth day in a row that she'd been sick, and she fully expected to feel better by midafternoon, just like all the other times.

At first she'd thought she was just coming down with something—a cold or the flu. She'd even considered that the headaches, nausea and tiredness were simply symptoms of stress due to her breakup with Mitch. Lord knew she'd been upset every one of the eight-and-a-half days since that night.

She'd left the engagement party right after he had, without bothering to go in and explain her absence to anyone else, and spent the rest of the evening crying into her pillow. If she had her choice, she'd still be crying, but since she hadn't wanted her father to begin to suspect anything was wrong, she'd cleaned herself up and tried to maintain a strong outer facade.

She would have to come clean eventually and admit to her father—and everyone else—that the wedding was off. But she just couldn't seem to bring herself to do it yet. Her emotions were still too raw, the pain still too deep and acute.

And judging by her father's comments and behavior, no one seemed to have a clue. They all thought she and Mitch were still engaged, still making plans to be married. Apparently, Mitch hadn't returned to the party or mentioned their split to anyone, either.

At the moment, though, that wasn't her biggest concern. She had worse problems than what people did or didn't know about her personal life.

Namely, she was late.

And now, she was beginning to believe she was in much worse trouble than just having to fight off the flu.

She was beginning to suspect she was pregnant.

Two weeks late for her period, morning sickness, moodiness and sensitivity…it might as well be written in neon across her forehead.

Then again, maybe she was wrong. Maybe she was overly emotional from the recent ups and downs with Mitch and was letting her imagination run away with her.

Meeting her reflection in the mirror above the sink, she noted the dark circles beneath her eyes and the sallow pallor of her skin.

There was only one way to find out if she needed an extra dose of vitamin C…or a bassinet.

She straightened away from the sink and stood perfectly still for a moment to be sure the room wasn't going to spin around her the way it so often did of late. Then, taking a deep breath, she opened the bathroom door and stepped out.

The house was quiet, and she sincerely hoped her father was busy outside so she could slip away without having to give an explanation or risk his noticing that she looked like the walking dead.

Grabbing her purse and keys, she slipped out the front door and headed for her car, which was parked only a couple of yards away. Just as she reached the driver's side door, her father stepped out of the barn and gave a shout of greeting.

"Morning, sleepyhead," he said, teasing her over her recent habit of waking up late, going to bed early and even taking naps during the day. "Where are you headed?"

"I need to run into town," she called back without elaboration. Then she yanked open the car door and jumped inside.

"Be back soon," she added before starting the engine and tearing down the drive so quickly, her rear tires sent gravel flying.

Pop would think she was crazy, she knew. Or at the very least, be very wary that something was wrong.

But how could she tell him that she might be pregnant? Even if she were happily married and had been attempting to procreate, the announcement would have made her blush. Telling him that she'd gotten herself in trouble *before* marriage and with a man who was now her *ex*-fiancé, would be positively mortifying.

A burst of hysterical laughter broke past her lips, and she blinked rapidly to keep tears from clouding her vision.

Dear God, how had her life gotten so out of control in such a short amount of time?

And what would she do if she really *was* pregnant?

Images of digging a deep, dark hole in the ground and burying her head in denial ran through her head. Oh, if only it were that simple. But if a baby was on the way, there would be nothing she could do to hide or refute the fact.

She made it to town in record time and aimed the nose of the car into the first available space near the drugstore. Leaving the keys in the ignition, she slammed the door and walked as fast as she could without breaking into a run.

Her breathing was labored by the time she reached the right aisle, from both anxiety and exertion. Rows of home pregnancy tests stared back at her, mocking her with their bright colors and promises of immediate results.

She wished even one of them promised the result she was hoping for. But life—and over-the-counter pregnancy tests—didn't work that way, and she had a sneaking suspicion this was one test she was destined to fail, no matter which brand she chose.

After studying the boxes a few moments longer, she grabbed one with a flashy yellow star announcing one hundred percent accuracy and headed for the checkout counter.

Relief washed through her when she saw a teenage boy behind the register. He wore a ratty black T-shirt advertising some heavy metal band she'd never heard of, his dirty blond hair stuck out in seventeen different directions, and he was leaning back against the cigarette rack reading an automotive magazine.

She didn't recognize him and prayed to God he didn't recognize her. If he did, word that Wyatt Davis's unmarried daughter had bought a home pregnancy test would likely spread through town like a brush fire. And that was one more problem she *did not* need.

Nose still buried in his magazine, the boy scanned the item without even glancing at it and stuffed it into a plain paper bag before checking the total and taking her money.

She carried her purchase out of the drugstore, stopping on the sidewalk for a split second and taking a deep breath before crossing the street and entering the local library. At this time of day, the place should be fairly empty. And she knew she could slip in, pretend to be perusing the stacks, then slip into the restroom at the back of the building and take this stupid test.

She smiled and said hello to Mrs. Alderson, the librarian, doing her best to shield the drugstore sack with her body. Making an effort to tamp down the urgency thrumming through her veins, she stopped at the New Arrivals section, then headed for the paperback rack, where she could disappear between the shelves.

Two minutes later, she was in the bathroom, peeing on a stick…and then she began to wait. With the little plastic wand balanced on the edge of the sink, she paced the tiny, tiled room and told herself not to panic.

She re-read the instruction sheet, checked her watch, read the instructions again. When she looked down at her watch a second time, her stomach plummeted.

This was it. The point of no return.

Stumbling forward, she closed the lid of the toilet and sat down, afraid she might fall otherwise once she got a glimpse of the results. With her eyes squeezed tightly shut, she reached over and grasped the plastic test strip. Holding it up in front of her face, she slowly opened her eyes…and was glad she was sitting.

Right there, in screaming aqua-blue was a plus sign as big as her thumb. *Plus means pregnant, minus means not pregnant.*

She was definitely, positively, plus-sign pregnant.

A wave of nausea rolled through her and she spent a long minute breathing through her nose until the sensation passed.

What in God's name was she going to do?

Emma didn't know how much time flew by while she sat there, numb, staring at the test wand in shock. But finally, she got shakily to her feet, grabbed her purse from the floor and stuffed both the pregnancy test box and the test itself inside.

Making as little noise as possible, she left the bathroom and stalked back between the shelves of books toward the front of the library. Mrs. Alderson was still behind the counter as she passed.

"Didn't find anything?" the woman asked politely.

"Nothing today," Emma forced herself to say in a voice that didn't tremble. "But I'll stop in again soon."

"All right, dear. Have a nice day."

Walking back to her car, she climbed in and started toward home. She wasn't even remotely ready to face her father—or anyone else, for that matter—but didn't know where else to go.

She thought about running away. To Europe or Hawaii or even just the other end of Texas.

But what good would that do? She didn't have the money to start over on her own somewhere else, even if she had been willing to leave her father and the only home she'd ever known. And at the end of the day, she would still be pregnant with Mitch Ramsey's child.

How could this be happening? She'd only recently begun to accept the fact that she and Mitch would never be more than just neighbors, and now this. Talk about a streak of bad luck.

Preoccupied, her mind swirling with a million scattered thoughts, she zipped past the turn to Mitch's ranch. A second later, she stood on the break, bringing her car to a screeching, skidding halt in the middle of the road.

She'd been going home—or at least heading in that direction—but now the idea of stopping off at Mitch's place first seemed to rise up and overshadow everything else.

Why should she be the only one plagued with this new knowledge? The only one suffering from a healthy mix of fear, panic, hysteria...

It was his child, after all. He'd played an equal part in its creation, however unplanned.

And—if she was feeling generous, which she was only about five percent of the time lately—she would admit he did have a right to know. Especially before she showed up in town with a growing belly, and word of her predicament got around.

Shifting the car into reverse, she backed up, turned right and drove slowly down Mitch's lane.

Her stomach was rolling, her palms sweating on the steering wheel. Lord, she wasn't looking forward to this. It had to be done, but she wished she could be anywhere else, doing anything else.

Pulling up in front of the house, she cut the engine and grabbed her purse off the passenger side seat. Her feet felt like lead weights as she crossed to the porch, wiping her damp palms on the legs of her jeans before lifting a hand to knock.

It was nearly lunch time, so she had a chance of catching him here. But if she had to, she would go out to the barn to look for him.

She was about to knock again when the inside door opened and she found Mitch standing on the other side of the outer screen door, staring down at her.

"Emma."

He sounded surprised to see her, even though his dark

eyebrows knit over storm-cloud eyes. It was obvious he still thought the worst of her.

Instead of bothering with pleasantries, she said simply, "We need to talk."

"About what?" The lines around his mouth lightened slightly, but he looked otherwise disinterested.

Reaching into her purse, she pulled out the test wand and held it up, big blue plus sign turned in his direction.

"What's that?" he asked.

"What does it look like?" she tossed back, her words laced with more than a little annoyance.

"I don't know," he drawled. "One of those fancy thermometers?"

Rolling her eyes heavenward, she heaved a frustrated breath. "No, not a thermometer. I wish."

Digging into her bag one more time, she came up with the flattened pregnancy test box. She waved it in front of his face, right beside the test stick.

"See this?" She was moving it back and forth so fast, he probably couldn't make out what it was, so she elaborated.

"This is a home pregnancy test," she said, thrusting the box against the screen. "And this is the little plus sign that means the test came out positive." She shoved that up right beside the other so there could be no confusion.

That, at least, elicited a reaction. The stern expression on his face washed away, replaced by a look of stunned disbelief.

"What…you mean…"

"I'm pregnant."

Mitch stared stupidly at Emma through the screen, then pushed the door open and moved onto the porch, forcing her back a step.

"You're pregnant," he repeated, feeling as though he was losing IQ points by the second.

"Yes."

She held out the pregnancy test pieces again, and this time he took the stick. That little blue plus sign she'd been talking about sure looked a hell of a lot bigger now. Ominously, toweringly bigger.

"When…" The word came out strangled and he stopped to clear his throat and lick his suddenly parched lips. "How did this happen?"

"The usual way," she snapped, fixing him with a freezing-cold, narrow-eyed glare. "And I'm not sure when. We were together a lot before calling it quits, and I guess we weren't quite as careful as we should have been."

He didn't say anything, still trying to wrap his mind around the fact that he was going to be a father.

A father.

He'd barely been ready to get married again, even knowing it was more as a favor and for the sake of convenience than anything else. The idea of having children had never occurred to him.

He'd thought that marriage to Emma would be easy and uneventful. One of those things that simply *was* and wouldn't require too much of his input or attention.

He'd been willing to marry her because her father had asked, but his decision had been underlined by the knowledge that they'd been friends since childhood and cared for each other already. Maybe not in the way most married couples cared for one another, but in his estimation it was a decent enough basis for a relationship.

It didn't hurt, either, that the sex was phenomenal. To him, that was an added bonus and one more sign that a marriage between them could work, even if there was no love involved.

When he'd pictured their future as man and wife, he'd seen them sharing a house, sharing a bed, working his ranch—and then someday her father's, too—together.

But nowhere in those pictures had he ever imagined children.

He probably should have. With all the sex he'd intended to have with her, the topic of pregnancy was bound to come up eventually. Emma might even have *wanted* children, which was another possibility he'd never considered.

In retrospect, he realized just what an oversight that had been. Of course, she'd have wanted children. Emma was a woman, and women loved kids.

But even if that had been the case, he'd have fought her on it. He had no idea what kind of father he'd make. The very idea terrified him. And having a child with her would only have risked evoking stronger emotions on Emma's part than he was ready to deal with, making more of their marriage than there was meant to be.

He scraped a hand over his face, stale air leaving his lungs in a huff of breath. The shock of her announcement was still reverberating through his system, chilling him down to the bone.

The Fates, it appeared, were having a field day. At his expense.

He'd been ready to marry her with no thought of children, even though they were a normal progression of an average marriage. Yet the minute they split up and despite all the precautions they'd taken to prevent this very thing from happening—at least after those first two hurried, spontaneous couplings—she wound up pregnant with his child.

Good God, what the hell was he going to do?

"Well," Emma prompted in a less-than-polite tone, her

fists propped angrily on her hips. "Don't just stand there. Say something."

If only he could *think* of something to say…other than asking again how the heck this had happened.

But then, he knew. The only question was how they planned to deal with it.

Clearing his throat to be sure it would work, he said the first thing that came to mind. "Why don't you come on in the house. I don't know about you, but I could use a drink."

He held the screen door open and waited for her to precede him inside. She did so reluctantly, her movements stiff, a mutinous expression on her face.

They headed for the kitchen and Emma took a seat at one end of the wide oak table while he took down two glasses from the cupboard and opened the refrigerator.

"What would you like?" he asked, leaning on the door to look inside. "I've got milk, orange juice, tea. Although you probably shouldn't have tea. I'm pretty sure it's caffeinated."

When he turned his head to glance in her direction, he found her arms crossed beneath her breasts and a frown marring her brow that was definitely aimed in his direction.

The problem was, he couldn't blame her. If she was half as mixed up about this new predicament as he was, then she had to be confused, scared, angry…basically tied in knots with no clue of how to untangle them.

He grabbed the jug of milk and poured her a glass, then poured tea for himself. But before he carried the drinks to the table, he opened another cupboard, pulled out a bottle of Jack Daniel's and topped off his tea.

"Sorry about this," he told her, replacing the cap and returning the bottle to its spot at the back of the shelf. "You could probably use a shot of this as much as I can, and it's not fair that you can't have any. But this is just going to have to be one of those things you hold against me, because if I don't get some liquor in me soon, I doubt I'll be much use to you at all."

Setting the milk down on the table in front of her, he pulled out another chair and took a seat, already downing half of his own drink in great, gulping swallows.

Not bothering to touch her own glass, she shifted slightly on her seat and said, "Aren't you going to ask me?"

He set his glass aside with a small clunk and met her bright, steady gaze. "Ask you what?"

"If you're the father."

The words hit him like a punch to the gut. Deservedly so, he supposed, after the way he'd acted at their engagement party.

He'd had no reason to suspect she was fooling around on him, especially with his own brother. But then, he'd never suspected Suzanne of cheating on him either, even though she'd been sleeping around almost the entire time they were married.

It was that knowledge, the realization that he could be blind to a woman's betrayal, that put him on his guard. No way in hell was he going to wind up married to another liar, another unfaithful woman.

So, yeah, he had trust issues. Anyone who knew him— or had known Suzanne was cheating on him, while he was left standing in the dark like an idiot—was aware of that.

But even with all of that hanging over his head, when Emma had told him she was pregnant, it had never once occurred to him that it might be another man's baby.

He didn't know why, except that just because a woman was *capable* of cheating didn't mean she had, and he simply didn't believe Emma had been sleeping with anyone else at the same time she'd been sleeping with him.

"No, I'm not going to ask. I don't think I need to."

If she found his behavior now odd as compared to the night of their broken engagement, she didn't say so. Instead, some of the tension seemed to seep from her body and her rigid posture began to relax. She sat up a bit straighter on the chair and leaned against the table, lifting her glass of milk to take a small sip.

Mitch took the opportunity to take another drink of his own odd mix, wishing it could be straight whiskey, even as the small amount in his tea warmed its way down his throat to his stomach.

"So how long have you known?" he asked quietly, concentrating on putting his glass back directly over the water ring it had left the first time.

She looked at her watch, then said, "About forty minutes."

He raised an eyebrow in surprise. Somehow he'd thought she'd had a few days to come to terms with this new turn of events.

"I haven't been feeling well," she explained, in answer to his unasked question. "After I'd been sick three or four mornings in a row, I started to think maybe I wasn't suffering from just a cold or a touch of the flu. I drove into town this morning, bought the home pregnancy test and took it in the bathroom of the library. Then I was on my way home and thought I should stop by to let you know…what was going on. It's bound to be all over town before long, anyway."

Her blue eyes flitted to the side, away from him, her fingertips worrying the rim of her glass. Then, without warning, the legs of her chair scraped the floor as she got abruptly to her feet.

"I don't want anything from you," she told him, backing through the kitchen and toward the door. "I didn't come here to make you feel guilty or rope you into anything. I just…thought you should know."

She'd reached the front of the house and stood with her back to the screen, one arm behind her, already pushing the door open a fraction.

"So I'll see you later. Have a good day."

Have a good day? Did she really think she could waltz up to his house, say, "Hey, I'm pregnant. Just thought you should know," and then waltz off again with a simple *have a good day?*

Uh-uh. Not with his child. Not while he still had breath left in his body.

"Emma," he called out, rising and moving to stand close enough that he could have reached out and touched her. To keep himself from doing just that, he stuffed his hands in the front pockets of his jeans and rocked back on his heels. His heart was pounding a mile a minute, sweat breaking out across his brow at the thought that was echoing through his brain.

"Yes?"

He blinked, bringing his attention back to Emma's face. Her soft complexion, bachelor's button eyes and wavy, strawberry-blond hair.

It might not be ideal. It might not even be what he really wanted. But it was right, and it was a necessary.

Lifting his gaze, he met her eyes, took a deep breath through flared nostrils and uttered the six words he knew would change his life forever.

"I think we should get married."

Eight

Emma managed not to snort rudely at this latest pronouncement of Mitch's, but just barely.

"We tried that once already, remember?" she muttered tiredly. "It didn't work out."

She saw the flash of memory cross his face and was struck with a fresh wave of pain at their short-lived engagement.

The muscles of his throat worked as he swallowed. "I think we should try again."

Closing her eyes for a brief second in weariness, she let her chin fall to her chest and then lifted it again. "Why?"

"Because you're pregnant, that's why."

Yes, because she was pregnant. Not because he was in love with her or wanted to be married to her but because she was pregnant. And, judging by the determined expression hardening his eyes and flattening his mouth, he wasn't going to listen to reason.

"This is my baby, too, Emma," he continued, apparently reading an equal amount of determination on her own face. "He—or she—should have my name and grow up with two parents who love and care for him. Or her."

He was trying, she knew that. And yet… "That's no reason to get married, Mitch."

"Around here, it is. You know how fast word will get around town that you're pregnant. You'll be labeled an unwed mother, and the baby will be labeled a bastard."

He pulled a hand from his pocket and moved it to the back of his neck, kneading as though trying to work out a particularly stubborn knot.

"Gabriel's Crossing is a good town, with good people living here, but we both know they can still be an opinion-ated, judgmental lot. They might never say anything to your face, but you know they'll whisper behind your back. Behind our child's back. How fair is that, to bring a child into this world with baggage like that to deal with?"

She shook her head, not because he was wrong, but because he was right…and the guilt trip was working.

Gabriel's Crossing *was* a good town, but it was also filled with citizens who held old-fashioned beliefs and values. And even though she didn't think any of them would truly treat her or an innocent child badly, Mitch was right about the gossip and the whispers. Eventually, in some way, their child would hear the word *bastard* or *illegitimate* and want to know what it meant.

Even if Mitch maintained an active role in their child's life, the stigma would still be there. And there was a difference between a father who was married to a child's mother and a father who dropped by once a week or picked the kid up for the occasional weekend visit.

"We can make it work," he pressed on, reaching a hand

out to touch her arm. "A lot of the wedding arrangements have already been made, and, unless you told people we broke up, no one even knows we called it off. We can go right back to being engaged and just move the date up a bit, if we need to."

He said it all so matter-of-factly, as though he were discussing his plans to buy a few more head of cattle. There was no emotion there, no eagerness or true desire to spend his life with her, merely his deep-rooted sense of responsibility that told him two people who were planning to have a child together should be married first.

She wished she could argue with him, offer a list of reasons his proposition was inferior to simply going on with their lives—separately, but sharing a child. The problem was, she had been raised the same way he had, with the same beliefs.

She didn't want to be a single mother. She didn't want to go home and tell her father that she was pregnant with Mitch's baby—but rather that the wedding was off. She didn't want to be the butt of gossip and condemnation, and she didn't want to raise her child on her own.

Mitch's thumb was making small, mesmerizing circles on the inside of her arm, distracting her even as his intense gray gaze burned into her, silently urging her to make the right decision.

If only he loved her, even a bit. The way she still loved him, despite everything. Childhood crushes, she supposed, were slow to die.

The worst part, though, was that she suddenly realized he'd never really felt anything for her. Not the way she'd hoped, at any rate.

Why he'd bothered to propose to her at all was a mystery. And she felt more than a little stupid for ever thinking she could help to heal his bitter, wounded heart.

Not that it mattered any longer. Necessity had taken the place of what either of them might have felt or wanted before. Now it had to be about the baby, about the best interest of their child.

As much as she hated the idea of being married to a man who didn't love her…or being married to a man who didn't *want* to be married at all…he was right about the need to give their child a name and let him or her grow up with a reputation free of labels or scandal.

Closing her eyes and feeling her shoulders slump slightly, she resigned herself to what she knew had to be done. She would sacrifice her own happiness, her own peace of mind for that of her unborn child.

Opening her eyes, she raised her gaze to Mitch's and prayed she wasn't making the biggest mistake of both their lives.

"All right," she said softly. "We'll go through with the wedding."

He didn't smile, but she felt the tension leave his body, loosening his muscles and lightening the rigid lines of his face.

"Good," he said with a firm nod. "We'll set the date as soon as possible and won't mention the baby to anyone before then. Agreed?"

"Agreed."

With that settled, she pushed backward through the screen door and stepped onto the porch. "I'll be seeing you, then," she said, heading toward her car.

He followed her across the yard. "Let me see you home."

"That isn't necessary," she told him, shaking her head and climbing behind the wheel.

Before she could slam the door closed, he caught it, rested an arm along the window frame and leaned over. "Is there *anything* I can do?" he asked quietly. "You know, about…" He waved a hand up and down to indicate her midsection. "Anything?"

She warmed a little at his offer and the obvious awkwardness that accompanied it. "No, thank you. I think we're okay for now."

"You'll let me know if that changes?"

"I'll let you know," she said, cocking her head to look at him, giving a small smile.

With a silent nod, he stepped back and closed the car door, then stood where he was while she started the car, turned around and drove off. She watched his unmoving form grow smaller in her rearview mirror as she headed down the long dirt driveway toward the main road.

She was engaged again, she thought, not sure whether to be relieved or disheartened. She was going to marry the same man she'd been set to marry before, the same man she'd fancied herself in love with.

Only two things had changed—she was pregnant, and this time she knew it was all for show.

Emma spent the next several weeks fighting morning sickness and making hurried wedding plans. Where they'd once intended to wed a few months or even a year down the road, the date had now been moved up significantly, the guest list whittled down to only family and very close friends.

Instead of getting married in the church, they were now going to exchange vows in his parents' backyard. They had made arrangements with the minister and rented a gazebo, folding chairs and most of the decorations that would make an outdoor ceremony complete.

Yet all of the things she should have enjoyed—deciding on flowers, addressing invitations, picking out a dress—

were merely duties to be done while pretending she was both nervous and excited about her upcoming nuptials.

In reality, she was just plain nervous. She was about to walk down the aisle in front of her father and friends and promise to love, honor and cherish a man she was marrying only to protect her unborn child.

She'd seen Mitch a handful of times since that day at his ranch when she'd told him about the baby. He was checking up on her, she knew, even though he'd never said as much, and they'd also agreed that they needed to be seen together both by their families and in town at least occasionally to keep up the pretext of being the happily engaged couple.

It hadn't been easy, and Emma was keenly aware that the rest of her life would be much the same—an act put on in public to convince people she was happier than she really was.

But she would have her child, she reminded herself.

Her hand slipped down to cover her still-flat abdomen. They would have each other, and she would do all she could to make her child's life a joyous one.

As for the rest…she would simply have to make the best of it.

A soft knock at the guest room door brought her head up, dragging Emma from her deep, dismal contemplations. She inhaled sharply and glanced in the mirror above the vanity table to be sure there were no telltale signs of her reluctance to walk down the aisle.

The door opened and Mitch's mother poked her head in.

"It's nearly time," she said with a gentle smile. "Your father is just outside, waiting to walk you down the aisle. Is there anything I can do to help?"

Not for the first time, Emma noticed in Theresa's face where Mitch had gotten his soulful eyes, high cheekbones and several shades of his dark, dark hair. The rest had come from his father, which only meant that he'd been twice blessed.

If all else failed, Emma thought, at least their child would benefit from the attractive gene pool on Mitch's side of the family.

Theresa stepped forward to fuss with the flowers in Emma's hair. Emma was wearing a plain white dress with no straps or sleeves, and more flounce in the knee-length skirt than she'd have liked. But there were only so many wedding dress options in downtown Gabriel's Crossing on such short notice.

She felt guilty enough even wearing white, considering her current condition and the things she and Mitch had done to get her there.

"I think I'm ready," she said, her voice somewhat scratchy with emotion and disuse.

Her future mother-in-law took a step back, still fingering the ends of Emma's reddish-blond hair, left loose around her shoulders.

"You look beautiful," she said, gazing at Emma with undisguised love and happiness. "My son is a very lucky man."

Unshed tears clogged Emma's throat and she fought to swallow them back. If Theresa only knew what a sham this entire ceremony was, she wouldn't be nearly so eager to see this wedding take place.

"All the guests are here and seated, and everything else is set. The only thing left is for the bride to make an appearance."

Taking a deep breath, Emma got to her feet. She smoothed the skirt of her dress, tugged the bodice up a fraction and reached for the bouquet of flowers at the edge of the vanity table. An assortment of simple wildflowers to match the blossoms in her hair, tied together with long strips of pale yellow ribbon.

"I'm ready," she murmured with a determined nod.

Theresa beamed, then opened the door and rushed out, leaving Emma to follow.

Her heart was pounding in her chest, fast and erratic, and her feet felt like bags of sand, dragging her down and slowing her steps.

As she rounded the corner from the guest bedroom, she spotted her father at the bottom of the stairs, dressed in a dark gray suit and grinning widely. She offered him her best reassuring smile and carefully descended the steps to meet him.

"I can't believe it's my little girl's wedding day," he said, his voice sounding suspiciously thick. Taking her hand, he lifted it to his mouth for a brief kiss. "You're just as pretty as a picture."

"Thank you."

"You remind me of your mother on our wedding day. She'd be so proud of you."

The mention of her mother immediately brought tears to her eyes, and she tipped her head back, hoping to keep her mascara from running.

She so wished her mother could have been there. Not just to see her get married, but as someone to confide in about everything that was going on in her life right now. Her mother was the one person she knew she could have talked to about Mitch, her unexpected pregnancy and this wedding that she knew neither she nor Mitch were a hundred percent ready to go through with.

But her mother was gone, and there was no one else to turn to. She had to do this, and she had to do it alone.

Forcing a smile to her face that she didn't quite feel, she let her father lead her to the rear of the house, with its wide-open back door. She could see the cloth aisle laid across the grass-sprigged yard and the rows of chairs covered with white fabric, filled with guests dressed in their Sunday best.

And there, at the end of that long aisle running between the two clusters of seats, stood Mitch beneath a white latticework trellis climbing with pink and white wild roses.

Her racing heart stuttered for a second as she studied him. He always had that effect on her—stopping her heart, slowing her breathing, sending her senses on red alert.

And today, he looked exceptionally handsome in his black suit and newly shined black boots. His black hair gleamed almost blue in the midmorning sunlight, and he'd spotted her. His intense gaze pinned her in the doorway, making her shiver.

Even though they weren't marrying for love, she had to admit that the lust was still there, at least on her part. One glance from those smoldering gray eyes, one touch of his strong, callused hands, and she was putty.

She only hoped he never figured that out or she would be in big, big trouble.

"Ready, sweetheart?" her father whispered, patting her arm where it linked with his.

Swallowing hard, she inclined her head, praying she made it all the way to the end of that long, long pathway without fainting or throwing up or screaming.

The music began, and everyone got to their feet, turning toward the house, waiting for the bride to begin her walk down the makeshift aisle.

Mitch watched Emma hover for a moment just inside the house, looking as though she planned to bolt, regardless of her father's hold on her arm.

He didn't blame her. If it weren't for his brother standing on his one side, the minister on the other and fifty of his closest friends and relatives seated all around, he might have made a run for it himself.

Not for the first time, he ran a finger around the inside of his too-tight shirt collar. Damn. He'd wanted to keep things simple and get this over with as quickly as possible, but he was beginning to think a daytime wedding, in Texas, in the middle of September, was a mistake. The sun was beating down like a heat lamp, threatening to make him sweat through his suit jacket before he even said "I do."

And Emma still hadn't moved. If she didn't come out of the house soon, people were going to start wondering just how eager she was to be marrying him.

Catching her eye, he smiled and gave her an encouraging nod.

That was all it took, it seemed, to jump-start her. She raised the collection of flowers that had been hanging at her side to the center of her waist and started forward, stepping onto the porch and then down into the yard, her movements in perfect alignment to her father's.

Despite her obvious reluctance, she looked lovely. He'd been through all of this before—albeit on a larger scale—but that didn't diminish Emma's natural beauty.

The simple white dress hugged her curves and left her slim shoulders seductively bare. Her wavy hair framed her delicate face, one side pulled up and held in place by the small bunch of flowers that matched those in her hands. The strawberry-blond strands shone like a new penny in the sun, and her skin glowed with a slight tint of pink beneath the surface.

She and her father reached the trellis and stopped. His eyes damp with emotion, Wyatt kissed her cheek and placed her hand in Mitch's with an approving nod before moving to take his seat in the front row of the folding chairs.

Emma turned more fully to face him so that they both

stood sideways directly in front of the minister, hands clasped between them. Her fingers squeezed around his, but he suspected it was more from nerves than as a gesture of closeness. Still, he squeezed back, offering what comfort he could and silently trying to let her know that everything would be all right.

They may not have planned for things to turn out quite this way, but they would make the best of it. They would have a child together and do their best to raise that child right.

And he would be a good husband. It might not have been his idea to get married again—not when her father had brought it up, at any rate—but he would still do the best he could to take care of her and see that she was happy.

The minister's words droned on, speaking of love and commitment. Things Mitch believed in but hadn't had much experience with—at least not the first time around.

He had no illusions that this time would be better. Emma was a different person, different from Suzanne in a lot of ways. But she was still a woman, and that meant she wasn't to be trusted.

Hadn't he caught her in his brother's arms the night of their engagement party? Seen it with his own two eyes. Both Emma and Chase claimed the embrace had been innocent. But he'd heard claims of innocence before and was no more sure he could believe them now than he could then.

Even if Emma and his brother were being honest…even if there had been nothing going on between them and never would be…he simply wasn't willing to take the chance. To open himself up to that vulnerability ever again.

But that didn't mean he couldn't be a good father and decent husband.

Finally, the minister had reached the important part.

"Do you, Mitchell Alexander Ramsey, take this woman to be your lawfully wedded wife?"

A few seconds later, after the rest of the vow, Mitch looked directly into Emma's cornflower-blue eyes, still clouded with uncertainty, and said firmly, "I do."

Emma slipped a ring on his finger and the minister asked her the same question.

"Do you, Emma Louise Davis, take this man as your lawfully wedded husband?"

She may not have looked certain and her fingers might have involuntarily contracted around his once more, but her voice didn't quaver as she answered.

"I do."

The minister pronounced them man and wife and, as he added that Mitch could kiss his bride, a cheer went up from the crowd of guests.

Before they were surrounded by well-wishers, he leaned in and pressed his lips to hers. To his surprise, she kissed him back, her delicate fingers curling into his forearms as she leaned closer.

As much as he might have liked to continue kissing her, he didn't care for an audience, and guests were moving in to hug them and pat him on the back. Reluctantly, he released her mouth, but kept her at his side, feeling oddly more comfortable with his new wife than he would have expected.

Nine

The wedding and small reception that followed went off without a hitch…if one didn't count the fact that neither the bride nor groom particularly wanted to be there.

Emma couldn't help but be amused by the irony of the situation as she left the reception—also held at Mitch's parents' house—with her new husband and headed for her place.

Or rather, her father's place now. It only made sense that after they were married she and Mitch would live together, and the obvious choice was for her to move to his ranch.

So, after dancing and eating and staying only as long as they felt necessary to keep up the pretense of the happy couple, they left to begin moving her things from one house to the other.

After three trips back and forth, she was exhausted, even though Mitch hadn't let her carry anything heavier than a grocery bag full of clothes and assorted toiletries at any one time. There was still a lot to go…larger things, like her hand-carved hope chest and a few sentimental items…but she had enough to get by. And if she discovered that she needed something, her father's ranch was only a couple of miles away.

Stifling a yawn, she made her way slowly upstairs, Mitch following close behind with his share of the last load. At the top of the stairs, she turned left and entered the extra bedroom, directly across from his own, where they'd been piling her possessions.

The bed was still clear, neatly made with a patchwork quilt coverlet, and as soon as she set aside the cloth tote she'd been carrying, she took a seat at the edge of the mattress. She was still wearing her wedding dress… another testament to Mitch's insistence that she not overdo it. He hadn't let her work hard enough to get so much as a smudge of dust on the soft white material.

"You look tired," Mitch commented from just inside the door. He leaned over to place the box in his arms on the floor before straightening to face her. "Why don't you take a nap."

It would certainly be easy enough to fall asleep. The stress and exertion of the day were taking their toll, making her eyelids droop and her limbs heavy.

But it was her wedding day. Technically, her wedding night, she thought, glancing at the bedside clock. It was barely 7:00 p.m.

When she didn't respond, Mitch tucked his hands into the front pockets of his black dress slacks, then tipped his head and left without another word, closing the door quietly behind him.

So much for being ravaged. Or passions overtaking them and spending a week in bed.

Hmph.

She fell back on the bed with a groan of frustration. There had been only one thing she was even remotely looking forward to in this marriage, and now it seemed Mitch intended to deny her even that.

Well, she'd just see about that.

Shaking off the traces of lethargy that urged her to stay in bed and drift off to sleep, she sat up and started digging through her bags and boxes of things. She knew she'd packed it. She even thought she'd put it somewhere on top for easy access.

"Ah-ha," she breathed when her hands closed on what she'd been looking for.

A slinky, satiny negligee, perfect for her wedding night. Or so she'd thought when she'd bought it on impulse soon after Mitch had asked her to marry him the first time.

Opening the bedroom door a crack, she looked out, checking for signs of Mitch. She didn't hear anything but noticed that his bedroom door—which had been open when they'd made all their trips upstairs—was closed. And the bathroom door was open.

She darted across the hall and locked herself in, setting the folded gown and robe on the closed toilet lid as she began to strip. First she removed the flowers from her hair, then reached behind her back to lower the zipper on her dress. Once she'd stepped out of the gown, she made quick work of her shoes, stockings, panties and bra.

Turning the water on in the shower, she stepped under the strong spray, quickly washing her hair and scrubbing every inch of her body. She wished she'd bothered to unpack some of her more feminine bath salts and hair care products, rather than having to make due with Mitch's all-purpose soaps. Maybe something in rose or lemon.

Then again, Mitch always smelled exceptionally good, and having his scent on her body from his soap was a decent substitute until—with any luck—she could get it to rub off directly from him.

She used a towel to create a turban for her hair, then rubbed herself dry with another. Once her skin was no longer damp and the delicate material of the negligee wouldn't stick, she shrugged the gown on over her head and checked herself in the mirror over the sink.

The cream-colored satin set off the red in her hair and the rosy hue the hot water had brought out in her skin. Quite a bit of skin had been left bare by the spaghetti straps and low, lace-trimmed bodice, too.

But that was the goal, after all. To leave just enough un-covered, and to wrap the rest in a seductive package to attract Mitch's attention.

With her hair hanging in damp tendrils around her shoulders, she slipped into the robe that matched the gown and ventured into the hall, leaving her other clothes behind. Mitch's bedroom door was open now, but there was no sign of him, which meant he was either downstairs or outside.

Feet bare, she padded down the steps, the hardwood floor creaking occasionally beneath her weight. As she reached the bottom of the stairs, she heard noises in the kitchen and headed that way.

Mitch was moving back and forth along the rows of cup-boards, putting dishes away. She stood in the doorway for a moment, watching him. Admiring his smooth move-ments, the sinewy flow of muscle in his back and arms.

He'd changed out of his suit and was now wearing his usual jeans and a plaid work shirt. A few stray pieces of straw clung to the cuffs of his pants, making her think he'd been out to the barn already.

But at least she'd caught him inside. It would save her having to either sit in the living room waiting heaven knew how long for him to return…or traipsing out there in her wedding night negligee, risking the lewd stares and ribald comments of his hired hands.

She wasn't sure she'd have actually had the courage to do the latter, so it was just as well he'd been out there and back already.

He turned from organizing silverware in the drawer beside the sink and spotted her. His gaze flitting from her head to her toes and back again, and for a moment his grip on the countertop tightened, turning his knuckles white. Then he let go and straightened, deliberately going back to what he was doing.

"Hey," he said, and she was delighted to hear a noticeable hitch in his voice. At least she'd succeeded in getting his attention, even if he was doing his best to ignore her.

"Hey, yourself."

He grabbed a couple of coffee mugs from the top rack of the dishwasher and moved to put them away. "I thought you were resting."

"I'm not tired," she told him, and prayed an ill-timed yawn wouldn't out her as a liar.

"Still, you've had a long day. You shouldn't overdo it."

She shifted slightly to rest against the framed opening that separated the kitchen from the dining area, aiming for a nonchalant pose.

"You had as long a day as I did," she pointed out.

He finished emptying the dishwasher and clicked the door closed with his hip.

"I'm used to it. And I'm not pregnant," he added pointedly, still leaning on the edge of the counter.

Well, he had her there. But she'd only spent the day getting married, not hauling horse feed or climbing Mount Everest.

"In case you missed it," she said, deciding to get right to the point, "this is our wedding night. We aren't supposed to fall asleep for quite a while yet."

Pushing away from the wall, she took a few slow steps forward until she stood directly in front of him. She held his gaze, but her fingers were busy teasing up and down the buttoned front of his shirt.

"But we can go to bed any time we like."

Going up on tiptoe, she pressed her lips to the underside of his jaw. It was like brushing against small grain sandpaper, even though he'd just shaved that morning.

She kissed his cheek, then the corner of his mouth, her fingers curling into the waistband of his jeans as she rubbed her body close to his, letting the friction build.

Only when she kissed him full-on, mouth to mouth, did she realize he wasn't responding. Oh, there was some definite action taking place below his belt buckle, but otherwise he held himself perfectly still, not moving, not kissing her back.

Pulling away slightly, she opened her eyes and looked up at him. His face was impassive, his lips drawn into a tight, flat line.

"Mitch?" She frowned, wondering if she'd done something wrong, been too aggressive for his tastes.

Wrapping his hands around her upper arms, he set her back a step. "You should get some rest. It's been a long day," he said without inflection.

She stood frozen in the middle of the kitchen, blinking in utter confusion. "Excuse me?"

"It's been a long day," he said for what had to be the hundredth time. "You look tired. You should be in bed."

So rather than making love to his new wife on their wedding night, he was telling her she looked *tired* and that she should go to bed *without him.*

She didn't know whether to be hurt or angry, but a fair share of both were building up in her bloodstream, threatening to send smoke shooting out of her ears. And all she could think to say was, "You're kidding, right?"

He gave a quick shake of his head, then busied himself with nonsense stuff around the room, like wiping down the already clean counter or moving the dish detergent on the windowsill an inch to the left.

"Get some sleep," he said, not bothering to meet her gaze. "I have some work to do in the barn."

And then he turned on his heel and walked out of the house. Leaving her alone. On her wedding night.

Mitch stalked straight across the lawn, climbed over the paddock fence and bent forward, immersing himself up to the shoulders in the cool water of the horse trough.

Dammit. Was she trying to drive him crazy?

It had been hard enough to resist her all day while she'd been dancing around in that snow-white dress that showed off her smooth, pale arms and drool-inducing legs. But did she have to get cleaned up and come downstairs in next to nothing?

She might as well have been naked. Oh, the robe and nightgown were long, running almost to her bare ankles, but the material was sheer and slinky and so thin, he could see the dusky circles of her nipples, the flare of her waist, the dark shadow between her thighs.

Her hair had been damp from her shower, and she smelled fresh and clean, with the scent of his soap clinging lightly to her skin. He'd gone hard in an instant, and it had taken every ounce of control he possessed not to take her right there on the kitchen floor.

And then, to feel those gentle curves pressed against him, burning through his clothes, her mouth hot on his own. He'd had to get out of there or risk doing something he'd regret, something he'd promised himself he wouldn't.

He *was not* going to sleep with his wife.

It was expected, he knew, especially on their wedding night, and Emma had made it clear she was more than willing. But to Mitch, touching her now felt too much like taking advantage of the situation.

She hadn't agreed to marry him this time because she wanted to but because she was pregnant. That didn't exactly make him feel like a typical groom.

He also didn't want to risk getting too close to her, physically or emotionally. Not after seeing her in his brother's arms and having all of his ex-wife's betrayals come flooding back.

And not now that they were legally joined, forced to live together. There was too much chance of getting more involved, of beginning to care too much. More chance than he was willing to take.

Keeping his distance was the best way he could think of to prevent that from happening and to prevent her from getting too attached or wrapped up in their sham of a marriage.

He lifted his head from the trough and shook himself, sending droplets of water flying in every direction. Stomping toward the side entrance of the barn, he ran his hands over his hair to squeeze out excess water.

The only problem with his brilliant plan, he thought as he entered the dim interior of the large, weather-beaten structure, was that Emma didn't seem to be on the same page as he was. She seemed more than willing to jump in with both feet and make this a real marriage, in every sense of the word.

And if she took it into her head to seduce him the way she'd tried in the kitchen…how the hell was he going to resist? How long could he hold out?

If his reaction to her today was any indication, not long. His blood was still simmering in his veins, his libido urging him to turn around, stalk back into the house and make love to his wife.

His gut gave a lurch at the image that popped into his head of Emma sprawled on his bed in that ivory nightie, writhing beneath him, curling around him. For a moment, he couldn't move, the longing thrumming so thickly through his system.

Drawing a deep, shaky breath, he forced himself to take a step forward and then another. He grabbed a bale of hay from the stack at the back of the barn and carried it closer to the empty horse stalls.

He would just have to be stronger, more determined. And he would have to avoid being near his new wife as much as possible.

Marriage, Emma decided, was not all it was cracked up to be.

She and Mitch had barely spoken in the month and a half since their wedding, and if they did it was only about the most mundane topics. The weather, the livestock, dinner with their parents. It was enough to make her want to scream.

Any time she tried to get close to him or even brushed close enough to touch as they passed in the hall, he acted like she'd scalded him with a burning hot brand. As often as not, he quickly made up some excuse to go out to the barn and get away from her.

He didn't seem to notice the changes her body was going through, either. They might not be major changes, but they were dramatic—at least to her.

Her pregnancy was starting to show in all the typical ways. Her breasts were growing larger and more sensitive, her stomach rounding out to a tiny mound that no longer fit beneath her pants unless they had an elastic waistband. And her tops, which used to be somewhat loose, were now snug, making her condition more obvious to anyone who cared to look.

Unfortunately, Mitch wasn't one of them. It was almost as though they were roommates—roommates who didn't particularly care for each other—instead of husband and wife. And it was beginning to get on her nerves.

Her father and Mitch's parents had been delighted at the news that they were going to be grandparents, though. And so far, none of them had brought up the fact that she was three months along in her pregnancy and only one month along in her marriage.

But even though it had only been six weeks since she'd exchanged vows and moved in with Mitch, she was becoming almost insanely bored. The few times she'd wandered out to the barn, hoping to find something to break up the monotony of her days, Mitch not only made it clear he didn't want her there, but if she so much as fondled the handle of a pitchfork, he immediately moved it out of her reach and reminded her that she was pregnant and shouldn't be working too hard.

Working too hard? She wasn't working at all. She was barely doing anything beyond cooking and keeping the already neat house free of dust and stray magazines. At least when she'd lived with her father, she'd had ranch business to keep her busy.

Maybe that's what she should do now that she was living here. Mitch spent so many hours outside, in the barn, working with the cattle and horses, she couldn't imagine he had much time for bookkeeping and organizing his records. He had a home office, complete with a computer monitor on the desk and file cabinets along the far wall, but she couldn't remember ever seeing him in there.

Of course, for all she knew, that could be where he spent his nights. It wasn't like they were sharing a room…or a bed.

But she still needed *something* to occupy her time and her quickly stagnating brain. So first thing that Monday morning, she got up, dressed and fixed breakfast as usual, not surprised when Mitch sat across from her, eating the food she'd prepared without speaking two words to her. She considered it progress that he grunted in response to a couple of her benign comments, uttered more to break the silence than because she actually expected any interaction with him.

Then, after he'd headed out the door, she made her way to his office and started snooping around. Not that she was looking for anything private or incriminating but to familiarize herself with his business.

Just as she'd suspected, he hadn't updated his records in quite a while. She found piles of receipts that hadn't yet been filed, as well as lists of livestock and records of sales and purchases.

Instead of being overwhelmed by the work that needed to be done, she felt a distinct sense of excitement. Finally, she had something to devote her time and attention to, a purpose for her married life other than being a so-called wife and glorified housekeeper. And maybe, if she was lucky, she might even prove herself to be an asset to Mitch and the Circle R.

It wouldn't solve all her problems… Heck, it might not solve any of them, especially where Mitch was concerned…but at least getting back to some office work would help her feel useful and keep her mind off of her miserable, failing sham of a marriage.

Ten

Two weeks later, Emma couldn't sleep. It had to be close to two in the morning, and rain was pelting the roof and windows by the bucketful, bringing with it the rumble of thunder and the occasional flash of lightning.

Normally, she enjoyed storms. The cool breeze, the relaxing rhythm of the rain, the fresh brightness and clean smell they brought to everything the next day.

But tonight, all those things only made her feel more alone.

With a sigh of defeat, she sat up in bed, threw back the covers and reached for her robe. Maybe a glass of warm milk would help.

Her slippers scuffed along the steps as she made her way downstairs and into the kitchen, turning on the dim light over the stove to illuminate the room without half blinding herself. She pulled a cup from the cupboard and the milk from the refrigerator, pouring enough for several healthy swallows before setting the heavy ceramic mug in the microwave and punching numbers.

While she waited for the buzzer to go off, she returned the milk jug to the fridge, then stood with her arms crossed, hip resting against the counter as she gazed out the front kitchen window. It was dark, the glass streaked and spattered by the rain, but still she could see a light on in the barn on the other side of the yard.

Her brow knit as she frowned. It was odd for anyone to be in the barn at this time of night—even Mitch, with the number of hours he spent trying to avoid her.

Out of curiosity, she wandered into the other room and halfway up the stairs until she could see his bedroom door standing open. She hadn't noticed it on her way past, but Mitch normally closed his door when he went to bed at night. The better to keep her out, she supposed.

The microwave beeped and she returned to the kitchen to retrieve her warm milk. As she sipped, she moved to the window to stare at the pale light showing through the half-open barn door, her curiosity piqued.

If Mitch wasn't in his room and didn't seem to be anywhere else in the house, that meant he very well could be out in the barn.

But why? She couldn't imagine any chores needing to be done so badly that they couldn't wait until morning. The obvious answer, of course, was an emergency with one of the animals.

Suddenly concerned, she set her mug on the kitchen table and moved to the front door. She slipped on a pair of tennis shoes and a jean jacket, then opened the door and ran out into the rain.

The ground was wet and muddy, the rain plastering her hair and clothes to her body almost the minute she stepped outside. She crossed the lawn in less than a minute, ignoring the soggy earth trying to suck down her shoes and splattering on her bare legs and the hem of her long nightgown.

Slipping through the crack in the barn door, she shook herself, wiped the water and clinging strands of hair away from her face, then glanced around to see if she could find Mitch.

The center of the barn was empty, filled with nothing more than the usual bales of hay, bags of feed and assorted equipment for cleaning stalls and currying the horses. But she heard noises at the far end of the building and started toward them.

One of the stall doors was open, and as Emma got closer she realized that what she'd heard was Mitch's voice, speaking in low tones. When she got close enough, she saw him hunkered over a dappled gray mare who was on her side on the stall floor, plainly in the final stages of giving birth.

Careful not to make a sound for fear she would distract him or disturb the horse, Emma stood at the edge of the stall and watched. Mitch continued to murmur encouragements, patting the mare's haunches and neck when he could, offering hands-on assistance when it was needed. In only moments, tiny hooves and a tiny nose appeared, and, when the time was right, Mitch tugged on the long, slippery legs to help pull the foal's body free of its mother.

On the final tug, Mitch fell back and the foal landed almost completely on top of him. Tears sprang to Emma's eyes as she heard his deep laughter and saw his wide smile as he made sure the foal's nose and mouth were clear, then helped get the baby on its feet.

The mare was back on her feet, too, licking the baby clean, and it only took a few minutes longer for the foal to start nudging around, searching for its first meal.

Mitch wiped his hands on the legs of his jeans and she quickly ran the back of her hand over her cheeks before he turned and caught her crying.

When he saw her, he froze for a second, then continued brushing the straw from his pants as he moved slowly toward her, his gaze raking over her body.

"What are you doing here?" he asked, stepping out of the stall, closing and latching the door behind him.

She shifted backward to stay out of his way, tugging the sides of her denim jacket closed and crossing her arms to keep them in place.

"I saw the light on and thought something might be wrong."

She glanced over the edge of the stall door at mama and baby, and he followed her gaze.

"Nothing wrong," he said, "just a mare in labor."

"I can see that." She smiled and stepped just a fraction closer. "He's beautiful. Or is it a she?"

"He. It's a colt."

Several seconds ticked by in silence while they watched the pair.

"You shouldn't be out here," Mitch told her, breaking into the moment. "You're soaking wet, and you should be in bed."

"I couldn't sleep." She turned, taking in his damp hair and the stains marring the front of his shirt and pants. "And I think you're in worse shape than I am."

He looked down at himself and grimaced. "Yeah, I guess a shower wouldn't be out of the question."

"Come on. Let's go back in the house." She slipped her arm through his, ignoring his protests that she would get dirty and tugged him forward. "I'll make us some hot cocoa while you get cleaned up."

Mitch turned out the lights and dragged the heavy door

closed before they set out across the yard at a jog. The rain soaked them through again and they hit the covered porch already shaking droplets from their hair and clothes. Just inside the door, they both kicked off their shoes and hung their jackets.

Emma padded barefoot across the kitchen and began digging in one of the low cupboards for the right size saucepan. When she realized Mitch hadn't moved from his spot by the door, she straightened to face him.

"You go ahead upstairs. Get a hot shower and change into some clean, dry clothes. I'll have the cocoa ready by the time you get back."

"Maybe you should take a shower first. You're just as wet as I am, and—"

She scowled and started tapping the bottom of the stainless steel pan in her hand against her leg. "If you say 'you're pregnant' one more time, I swear, I'll bean you. Yes, I'm pregnant, but no, that doesn't mean I'm as fragile as a china doll. It hasn't started to get cold out yet, and a little bit of rain isn't going to kill me. I'm not even cold, and I'll dry. You, however, are both wet and dirty. So go."

His eyes darted to the pan at her side, then back to her face, apparently reading the annoyance there quite clearly. He stuffed his hands in the pockets of his jeans, his shoulders slouching forward just a touch.

"Right. I guess I'll go get that shower then."

Struggling not to laugh, she forced her mouth to remain tight, knowing that he would hear the amusement in her voice even if her expression remained stoic. "Good idea."

He spun on one stockinged foot and marched out of the entryway in the opposite direction. She listened to the squeak of boards and the sound of his footfalls as he passed through the living room, then up the stairs.

When he reached the bathroom and she began to envision him stripping out of his damp clothes, down to nothing but skin, she knew she had to get busy making the cocoa or risk melting into a puddle in the middle of the kitchen floor.

He might have made it clear he had no interest in sleeping with her, but that didn't mean her hormones had gone off to hibernate. If anything, they were more charged and raring to go than ever. She blamed it on pregnancy, sending her libido into overdrive.

Or maybe it was simply a matter of wanting something even more once she'd been told she couldn't have it.

Either way, looking at him made her feel like a dieter faced with an all-you-can-eat dessert buffet. She was famished, salivating and more than ready to cheat.

She winced, then blew out a huff of breath and turned for the stove. That was probably not the best analogy, considering Mitch's biggest fear was just that—that she, or any woman he got involved with, would cheat on him.

But while she was definitely eager to cheat on her no-sex diet, she would never, ever cheat on him.

Even if he never touched her again. Even if he insisted that their marriage remain a cold, passionless one.

She might have to resort to a dozen cold showers a day or investing in a battery-operated self-pleasuring device, but she would never be unfaithful. Not when it was the one thing that would hurt Mitch the most.

And regardless of anything else going on between them or in their lives, that was something she would never intentionally do.

Measuring out milk, sugar and cocoa powder, she mixed them together in the saucepan and set it on a burner over low heat. Just about the time the water turned off upstairs and she heard him moving around again, the cocoa was ready. She turned off the stove and took down an extra mug, filling both with steaming chocolate.

Before setting the drinks on the table, she dropped a few slices of bread in the toaster and pressed the lever. A minute later, Mitch came down the stairs and reappeared in the kitchen doorway.

His hair was still wet, but this time, she assumed, from being freshly washed. And, instead of changing into pajamas or boxers, he'd opted for another pair of denims and a long-sleeved plaid work shirt. He was barefoot, though, and had left the tail of the shirt out rather than tucking it into the waistband of his jeans.

A jolt of awareness zinged through her body, settling warmly between her legs. Swallowing hard, she made a mental note to do some discreet online shopping…and pick up extra batteries the next time she was in town.

But outwardly she tilted her head toward the table and smiled. "Cocoa's ready. And I'm making toast to dunk. I don't know about you, but I love hot buttered toast with my cocoa."

Without saying a word, he passed behind her and took a seat, wrapping his hands around the still-hot coffee cup. She thought about warning him not to burn his mouth, then decided he was a big boy and could certainly tell by the temperature of the ceramic mug and the steam emanating from the liquid inside that it was too warm to drink right away.

The toast popped and she buttered it, then cut the slices in half before setting them on a plate and carrying them to the table. She sat in the chair nearest him, put the plate between them and reached for her own cocoa.

Mitch watched Emma drifting around the kitchen, as comfortable and proficient as ever. Almost immediately after moving in, she'd made herself at home as though she'd always lived under his roof.

Without a word of discussion, she began cooking three meals a day and tidying up. He'd even had to phone his once-a-week housekeeper on the sly and ask her not to come until further notice. He didn't want Emma thinking he didn't appreciate her efforts or that she wasn't doing a good enough job. Especially when he was well aware there was too little to keep her busy around the place otherwise.

Although he made a point not to be around her any more than he had to, he'd noticed the work she'd done in his office and was secretly glad. Not only that she had found something she enjoyed to occupy her time but that she'd taken it upon herself to deal with a part of the ranch business he hated. From what he'd seen, she had managed to organize and complete all of the bookkeeping he had been avoiding for weeks.

Having her here, taking over so many household duties, was somewhat disturbing. It was almost too domestic for his tastes, too strong a reminder that he and Emma really were married and likely to stay that way for a hell of a long time, regardless of the circumstances.

But it wasn't Emma's ability to make a damn fine cup of coffee or balance his books that set him most on edge. It was *her.*

Her presence. Her voice and her scent. Her hair and the sound of her footsteps as she moved around the house. The way she sometimes hummed while she cooked, or the warm, steamy feel of the bathroom after she finished one of her long bubble baths.

Everything about her heated his skin and sent his temperature rising. He awoke each morning with the smell of her in his nostrils, so strong he could swear she'd spent the night beside him in bed.

And her body…her body was enough to make a godless man pray. Especially now, with the changes her pregnancy was making.

They were subtle, to be sure, but he noticed every last one. The slight swell of her small breasts, the gentle rounding of her formerly flat abdomen.

And he wanted, more than anything, to rest his hand on her stomach and feel the place where his child was growing. He dreamed of it, ached with it.

But touching her even that much, to share in the development of the baby they'd made together, would be too dangerous. Because he knew that one touch of her belly would never be enough. He would want to touch her face and her neck and work his way down. He would want to kiss her and make love to her.

As it was, he lay awake at night, remembering what it had been like to hold her, caress her, be inside her. Before, when their relationship had been casual instead of complicated, temporary instead of permanent.

He lifted his mug with both hands and took a long slug of hot chocolate, wishing it were something ice-cold to cool his ardor. Not that it would make much difference. With Emma around, he was in a constant, near-painful state of arousal.

In between bites of toast and sips of cocoa, she was talking about the new colt that had just been born. Her voice was light and upbeat. It washed over him and soothed his jagged nerve endings, even as it turned him on.

She had that effect on him. Hand in hand with his desire for her came a deep level of comfort. Like a roaring fire on a cold winter's night or the kind of ease he would expect to feel after living with someone for fifty years.

But it had always been that way with Emma. Maybe because they'd grown up together and had seen each other through the chicken pox and gawky teen years, broken bones and broken hearts.

Or maybe it was just Emma, with her soft smile and kind eyes and her gentle demeanor that seemed to accept everyone for who they were, warts and all.

And God knew he had enough warts for a garden full of toads. It hadn't always been that way, but it sure as hell was these days. Frankly, he didn't know why she'd gotten involved with him in the first place, let alone agreed to marry and move in with him.

"Mitch?"

He blinked, suddenly aware that her stream of chitchat had ended and she was looking at him as though waiting for an answer.

Shaking his head, he set his cup on the table with a small clunk and said, "Sorry, guess my mind drifted there for a minute. What was the question?"

She smiled and shook the hair back from her face. It was still damp from the storm, falling in dark, stringy strands around her shoulders.

And her hair wasn't the only thing that was damp. Though they'd been indoors for nearly half an hour, her long white nightgown was still wet in patches. The thin cotton material had been no real barrier to the pounding rain, and despite her claims that she wasn't cold, her nipples had beaded into tight, rosy points.

He could see them clearly through the transparent fabric. Or perhaps it was just his imagination, his memory of how her breasts looked, felt in his hands, tasted against his lips and tongue.

Dammit, he was as stiff as a fence post. If the wide tabletop hadn't hidden the lower half of his body from view, Emma would no longer have had a single doubt about his feelings for her. He may have been able to *tell* her he wasn't interested with a straight face, but his physical response to her was bound to give him away if he wasn't careful.

Inhaling and exhaling with almost surgical precision, he fought to get his longing under control. His fingers tightened around the mug in his hands until the knuckles turned white, and he made himself meet Emma's gaze head-on rather than drifting toward her alluring chest.

"It was nothing," she said, still smiling, oblivious to the war that was raging in his bloodstream. "I was rattling on about nothing very important."

And then she stood, carrying her empty cup to the sink. "You're probably tired and don't need to stay up with me just to be polite."

While she rinsed her mug and brushed crumbs from the plate she'd used for toast, Mitch seized the opportunity to rise from the table. With her back to him, he could slip out and away before she noticed the rather prominent bulge in his jeans.

"Here you go," he said, standing as far away as possible while at the same time reaching around to set his own mug in the sink.

His plan was to dump the glass, then hightail it out of the kitchen and up to his bedroom, where he could lock the door and be safely away from Emma's unintentional seduction.

But at the same moment glass clinked on stainless steel, she turned, the front of her body coming flush with his own.

The tiny expanse of her belly brushed just above his belt buckle, the loose fabric of her gown across his groin, and he groaned. It was like setting a hot branding iron to naked flesh. In a flash, his diaphragm clenched, his heart lurched and his blood reached the boiling point.

Her blue eyes stared up at him, wide open and swimming with an odd mix of uncertainty and longing.

He swore, cursing himself for being the one to make her doubt her beauty, her desirability. He'd meant to keep his hands off of her, yes, but never to lessen her self-esteem or self-assuredness.

She was beautiful, amazing. Any man would be lucky to have her. He just happened to be the poor sap who'd gained her affection when he was neither worthy of nor able to return her feelings.

"Emma..." He ran a hand over her tangled hair, cupping the back of her head in his palm.

Her tongue darted out to lick her lips and he almost exploded. He pressed closer, rubbing sensually against her where he needed her touch the most.

In a soft, shaky voice, she whispered, "I thought you didn't want me anymore."

With a moan, he let his head drop until their brows met. "I always want you," he told her in a gravelly voice. "I didn't *want* to want you, I tried to fight it, but it's still there. Every day, every night, awake or asleep. I've taken more cold showers since you moved in here than ever before in my life, and not a damn one helped."

Her eyes welled and for a moment he feared she was about to burst into tears.

"You could have fooled me," she said with a hint of anger, her tone stronger and more confident than before.

"I *tried* to fool you. I tried to fool myself. But this doesn't lie." He pushed the hard ridge of his erection into the apex of her thighs, letting her know exactly how much he craved her.

Something flashed in her eyes for a brief second, a hint of lust to match his own. But then she tamped it down and her expression grew serious.

"What if I told you that I'm only willing to sleep with you if I know you love me and are serious about making this marriage work?"

His jaw clenched, his fingers tightening where they wrapped around her delicate forearms. "I'm serious about making this marriage work," he responded carefully.

"But you don't love me."

She said it matter-of-factly when he would have expected her to make it sound more like an accusation. Before he could answer, she shrugged a slim shoulder and a ghost of a smile began to play on her lips.

"It's all right," she told him. "If you'd said you did, I'd have known you were only doing it to get me into bed. At least this way, I know you're being honest with me."

"I've never lied to you," he said firmly. There may have been a few occasions when he hadn't told her the entire truth, but he'd never lied.

She leaned closer, letting the heat of her body mingle with his and running her hands over the taut muscles of his biceps.

"If we do this," she said in a low voice that poured over his skin like aged whiskey, "there's no going back. Consummating our marriage means we can't get an annulment if we change our minds in a few weeks. We would have to divorce."

"The thought never entered my mind," he told her truthfully. "And there won't be any divorce. When I said 'till death do us part,' I meant it."

He'd married her for better or worse, with his eyes wide open. It may not have been for love, may only have been to give their child a stable home and protect Emma's reputation, but he'd always intended it to be a forever thing. No matter what.

Her fingers moved from his shoulders to the back of his head, tangling in the short strands of his hair. "Then I guess it's about time we had our wedding night."

Eleven

She lifted her mouth to his, sighing with contentment as their lips met and he kissed her like she was a bountiful oasis and he was a man left too long in the desert without a drop to drink.

His hands framed her face as his mouth threatened to devour her. She might have been frightened by the desperation in his kiss, his touch, if she hadn't been equally desperate and aroused.

Without breaking the kiss, he stroked down the sides of her throat, over her breasts, coming to rest with his hands on the slight swell of her abdomen. His thumbs moved up and down as though testing the shape and texture of her expanding figure.

He pulled away, his chest heaving with each ragged breath he struggled to take into his lungs. She was gasping, too, and shaking so hard she was surprised she was able to stay on her feet.

"Is it all right?" he asked. "With the baby…is it all right if we do this?"

"Oh, yes." She ran her hand over the rough line of his bristled jaw and smiled encouragingly. "It's fine, I promise. You won't hurt either one of us."

"Thank God."

It was the most heartfelt declaration she'd ever heard from him, and she might have laughed if he hadn't leaned in and scooped her off her feet so fast, all she could do was yelp and hold on tightly.

"What are you doing?"

"Taking you to my room," he told her, his long strides eating up the floor as he stalked through the kitchen, dining room and up the stairs, carrying her as effortlessly as he would a bag of grain.

"Ever since you moved in, I've dreamed of having you in my bed. I can't sleep at night for wanting you so bad."

"I was right across the hall," she whispered softly, using her teeth and tongue to tease the lobe of his ear. "Why didn't you ever come over and get me?"

"I was trying to do the honorable thing." He groaned low in his throat, a sound that came much closer to a growl. "Dammit, I didn't want to use you. Just because we had to get married, I didn't want you to think I was taking advantage of you."

"It's not taking advantage if I want you back," she said as they reached the bedroom and he kicked the door closed behind them, heading directly for the wide, king-size bed.

The covers were pulled down and tangled, as though he hadn't made the bed in several days. Not that she cared. She had a feeling the sheets would be in much worse shape by the time they finished with them.

"In the morning, I hope you'll remember you said that."

Because I am going to make love to you tonight, and I won't regret it for a second, even if you think I should."

He set her gently in the center of the bed, before stepping back to loosen his belt and pop the buttons of his shirt. Shrugging his arms out of the sleeves, he let the soft plaid flutter to the floor, then went to work on the front of his jeans. He shoved the denim and his underwear down his legs, kicking them aside.

He strode back to her, delectably naked and fully aroused. She only had a moment to appreciate his long legs and broad, muscular chest before the mattress dipped and he was stretched out beside her, kissing her lips and caressing the flesh of her arm, left bare by her sleeveless nightgown.

His fingers trailed upward, around the lacy edge of material near her collarbone, then over the rise of her breast to the line of tiny pearl buttons lining the front of her gown.

As he began slipping them through their holes, he lifted his head and murmured against her mouth, "Did anyone ever tell you how beautiful you are? And that you have lousy taste in sleepwear? These buttons are too damn small."

Her heart leapt at his compliment, then settled back in her chest as she chuckled at his complaint. If she'd known the evening was going to lead to something as wonderful as this, she'd have worn a robe—and not a stitch more.

"Please tell me this isn't one of your favorite nighties," he said, his head bowed now as he concentrated. He had six buttons undone and was still only halfway down her chest.

"No, not at all, it's just—"

"Good. I'll buy you another one, I swear."

And then the sound of tearing filled the room, followed by the soft ping of tiny plastic buttons hitting the floor, headboard, nightstand. Cool air hit her chest as he laid her bare. When he moved to push the gown down her arms, she sat up to help him, then lifted her hips and legs so he could get rid of the offending garment altogether. It landed on the floor near his own pile of quickly discarded clothes.

He covered her once again with his own long, hot body, and she wrapped her arms around his back, loving the feel of his warm, smooth skin beneath her hands, his hair-roughened chest abrading her nipples, the hard, throbbing length of him pressing between her legs.

She opened for him, more than ready to take him inside her. Yearning for it, aching with all the pent-up passions she'd been struggling with since their ill-fated wedding night.

But Mitch seemed to be in no rush. Instead, he kissed her, ran his hands through her hair, over her breasts. His thumbs teased the tightened peaks until she writhed beneath him, and then he followed the action with his lips. His tongue licked and swirled before he drew the entire tip into his mouth to suckle.

She whimpered, holding tightly to the back of his head even as the sensations became almost too painfully pleasurable to bear.

With one final swipe, he moved away, only to stare down at her with his own dark, smoky-gray gaze.

"They're bigger. Not by much, but I could tell just by looking. The same here."

His hand moved down to cover her belly and a shiver of awareness rippled through her.

"The baby's growing." With his eyes still locked on hers, he said, "Do you have any idea what that does to me? Watching your body change, knowing I played a part in it?"

He slipped down until his face hovered just above her abdomen. Leaning in, he pressed his lips to the minor bulge, then lifted his head and grinned. "I've been wanting to do that for weeks now."

She returned his smile, blinking rapidly and swallowing hard to keep emotion from clogging her throat. "I've wanted you to do it."

That and so much more. She'd wanted him to touch her, kiss her, hold her. She'd wanted to fall asleep in his arms and wake up the same way. She'd wanted to talk with him and laugh with him and share some of the changes her body was just beginning to go through.

And now he was doing at least some of those things. It gave her hope and lifted her spirits for the first time in months.

He continued to dribble soft, ticklish butterfly kisses over her stomach before moving lower. She squirmed, suddenly shy, and tried to pull him back up by tugging at his hair. But he ignored her, continuing his quest and shifting her legs so her thighs were balanced on his shoulders.

She pushed up on her elbows, attempting to slide backward, away from what she thought he was trying to do. "Mitch, you don't—"

Slapping the side of one bare buttock playfully, he raised his head and gave her a determined, lascivious look. "Hush. This is something else I've been dreaming about, and you're going to let me. All you have to do is lie back and enjoy."

The first touch of his mouth on her warm, swollen flesh set off bursts of color behind her closed eyelids. Her fingers curled in the sheets on either side of her hips as she panted in pure, unadulterated pleasure.

His tongue licked, stroked, flickered and swirled. He started slowly, then sped up, bringing her to the precipice of climax before slowing down again and making her whimper.

When he began to concentrate on the tiny bud of desire buried within her slick folds, she didn't even try to hold back but let the sensations overtake her.

Her body bowed, lifting off the mattress for several long seconds before her bones melted like hot candle wax and she slumped back down. She was breathing hard, amazed that she'd managed to remain conscious.

Mitch pushed himself up, a smug, self-satisfied smile curling the corners of his mouth. "Can I take that to mean you enjoyed yourself?"

She made a noise that might have been a laugh, but even she wasn't sure. Grabbing him by the ears, she yanked him up until they were once again face-to-face. "Shut up and kiss me, you big jerk."

His chuckle of amusement was swallowed by her lips. She tasted herself on his tongue and moaned, letting her hands drift down his sides and between their sweat-slick bodies. Her fingers closed around his stiff, pulsing member and it was his turn to gasp and writhe.

She teased him, running her hand back and forth, squeezing, skimming the pad of her thumb over his sensitive, dew-kissed tip.

Finally, he grabbed her wrist, putting a halt to her erotic ministrations. "That's enough, I can't take anymore."

"You did it to me," she shot back.

"Yeah, but I can't recover as quickly as you can, and I want to be inside you when I come."

With that, he got to his knees and sat back on his haunches, pulling her up with him. She was poised directly over his rampant erection, and as she crossed her legs behind his back, she slipped down, taking him into her eager, waiting body.

They both sighed at the glorious friction their joining created, remaining still for a moment to let the ecstasy pour through them. And then his hands closed on her buttocks. He lifted her slowly and she watched a muscle in his jaw jump at the same time the muscles in his arms rippled and bulged.

He let her down slowly, only to lift her again, then let her down. Over and over until her limbs quivered, her belly contracting with the anticipation of what was to come.

She dug her nails into the meat of his shoulders as her inner sheath tightened around him with the first signs of orgasmic spasms. Mitch's lips peeled back from his teeth, telling her he wasn't far behind. With her heels digging into the mattress, she rose and fell on him faster and faster, while his hips tilted to meet her thrust for thrust.

In a flash, the building pressure reached its limit and spilled over. Beneath her, he tensed and gave a low growl of completion. A second later, she followed him over the edge with a keen cry of her own.

For long minutes, they stayed that way, the sounds of their ragged breathing filling the room. Then he circled her waist with one arm and carefully lowered her back to the mattress.

She almost groaned in disappointment when he slipped out of her, but he quickly rolled to his side, drew the covers up over them both and hugged her close.

Feeling happier than she had since the first time he'd proposed, she fell asleep cocooned in his warmth, wishing she could whisper the three words singing through her soul.

I love you.

The moment Emma opened her eyes early the next morning, she knew something was radically different. It took a few seconds for the fog to clear from her brain and the previous night's events to come flashing back.

As soon as they did, a wide smile split her face and she started to stretch. *This* was what she'd expected marriage to be. *This* was how she'd wanted to feel on her wedding night and every day thereafter.

"It's about time you woke up."

The low, rumbled voice near her ear made her jump. Only then did she feel the strong male forearm around her waist as Mitch drew her back against his chest, which vibrated with laughter.

"I expected you'd be out at the barn by now," she said, tipping her head until his face came into view. His gray eyes sparkled and a dark shadow lined his tanned jaw.

"I thought about it but couldn't seem to drag myself out of bed without you."

Goose bumps broke out along her skin at his words. This was a side of him she'd never seen before, playful and romantic.

"Won't the cows get hungry without you?"

He chuckled. "Nah. I've got hired hands to pick up the slack."

She rolled the rest of the way around, mimicking his position of propping her head on one bent arm. Beneath the covers, their legs rubbed together and she could feel her blood begin to heat.

"Does that mean you're taking the day off to stay in bed and satisfy your sorely neglected wife?"

One black eyebrow winged upward. "After last night, can you really say you've been neglected?"

"No, I suppose not." Her cheeks heated at the memory of the things they'd done together each of the three times they'd awakened throughout the night. "But if you abandon me now, I might."

His hand moved from the small of her back to the curve of her bottom and he pulled her close so she could feel his arousal growing between them.

"Well, we can't have that, now can we?"

His kiss set off brush fires in her bloodstream and it was a long, long time before either of them made any attempt to get out of bed.

Hours later, they were downstairs. Showered, dressed and full from a quick brunch that they'd prepared together between feather-light touches and lingering kisses.

Mitch's hand enfolded hers on the table all the while they ate, and then, after his last sip of coffee, he gave a heavy sigh and pushed back his chair.

"As much as I hate to, I really should go out and check on things. Would you mind?"

The way he'd been acting since last night, she wished he would stay with her forever. Right there, touching her, kissing her, looking at her with such attentive devotion in his storm-dark eyes.

But she knew how implausible that was and knew, too, that if she clung too tightly to him, there was a chance he'd begin to feel smothered and pull away.

So as much as she didn't want to, she smiled and shook her head. "Of course not. Do you need any help?"

He stood, still holding her hand and pulling her to her feet. "I don't need help, no. And half of what I'll probably end up doing, I wouldn't let you take part in, anyway. Not in your condition."

The corners of his lips lifted in a gentle grin and his free hand slipped down to caress her belly through the layers of her slacks and top.

"But you're welcome to come out and see the new colt, if you want. Just make sure you wear boots and are careful around the mare. New mamas can get nasty if they think their babies are at risk."

She nodded, reaching up to meet him as he leaned down

to kiss her, then walking him to the door. He threw her one last smile over his shoulder before crossing the lawn and disappearing into the barn.

As she walked back to the kitchen and started clearing the table, Emma caught herself humming. With any luck, Mitch wouldn't get cold feet again, and they could go on like this indefinitely.

He may not be in love with her, but phenomenal sex and a positive outlook could make up for a lot. They certainly respected each other and would soon have a child to bind them together even more.

She could be happy with that, she told herself. And only a very small voice in the very back of her mind whispered, *But maybe not forever.*

For now, though…for now, she was more than willing to take it day by day.

She finished in the kitchen and wandered back to Mitch's office, deciding to spend a few minutes dealing with paperwork before heading out to the barn. If she waited long enough, perhaps Mitch would be done with his work and could join her in admiring the newborn foal. She liked the idea of watching the baby together, knowing that they would soon have a baby of their own to share.

By the time she glanced up from the computer screen, an hour had passed. She rubbed her eyes and rolled her neck to work out the kinks, then pushed back the wheeled desk chair and hopped to her feet.

Mitch would surely be finished by now, or close to it. Hurrying to the front of the house, she stepped into her old, worn work boots and opened the front door.

A woman was standing on the porch just in front of her, hand raised to knock.

Emma gave a gasp of surprise and stepped back, then

felt her stomach lurch as she recognized the overly bleached, violently teased hair. The skintight, hot-pink, scooped-neck top revealing entirely too much cleavage. The white, painted-on spandex pants and bloodred toenails sticking out of three-inch high, platform slides.

It was Suzanne. Mitch's ex-wife and *the first* Mrs. Ramsey.

Twelve

Emma felt the earth lurch beneath her feet and her lungs seize painfully in her chest. She reached out a hand, grasping desperately for the doorjamb to catch herself before she fell over.

What in God's name was Suzanne doing here?

Why now, just when everything seemed to be going so well?

Crossing her arms beneath her well-endowed breasts, Suzanne hitched her hip and scowled. "Who the hell are you?"

The rude demand snapped Emma out of her near-catatonic state and was like a dousing with ice-cold water. She shook herself mentally and straightened her spine, now using her grip on the doorframe to keep from clawing at the woman on the other side of the screen.

"I'm Emma. Emma Davis," she said, using her maiden

name, since she thought it might be one Suzanne would recognize more easily than her married name. "We've met before at—"

Suzanne's gaze slipped past Emma to look deeper into the house before she'd even finished speaking. "Where's Mitch? I'm his wife and I want to see him. Where is he?"

Emma's eyes narrowed and an angry heat swept up from the soles of her feet. She fisted her hands at her sides, furious not only at the woman's obvious dismissal of her presence but at her false claims of being Mitch's wife.

"*Ex*-wife," Emma said just above a growl, surprised her teeth didn't shatter from the force with which she was grinding them together. "You're his *ex*-wife, Suzanne."

"Not for long," the woman replied lightly, tossing back her peroxide-enhanced hair. "The divorce was just a phase, one of those things newlyweds go through. We'll reconcile and be remarried in no time."

"Sorry to disappoint you," Emma said, still seething, "but that might not be as simple as you think. You see, *I'm* Mitch's wife now."

Suzanne's mouth fell open, her eyes flashing fire, and Emma braced herself for a knockdown drag-out. The screen door still separated them, but she had no illusions that the thin barrier would keep Mitch's ex out if she decided to go for Emma's jugular.

Nor was she afraid. She'd been raised on a ranch and suffered her fair share of kicks from horses and cows both, as well as falling out of trees, the loft, off the back of tractors. Fighting might not be something she was used to, but she could certainly handle herself, especially against one puffed-up, painted-on floozy.

But before Suzanne could respond or Emma could slam

the door in her face, Mitch's voice rang out from the center of the yard.

"I thought I heard a car in the drive. Do we have company?"

Emma had to lean to one side to see around Suzanne's big hair. Mitch's long strides were eating up the ground, but his head was down, the brim of his hat hiding his eyes and obscuring his view as he tugged off his leather work gloves.

He apparently didn't recognize Suzanne's car or he would have known immediately who their "company" was.

With his booted foot on the bottom porch step, he lifted his head and spotted Suzanne for the first time. His eyes went wide in startlement, and Emma almost expected his mouth to drop open like in the cartoons.

She found his reaction reassuring. Despite her own annoyance at his ex's unexpected arrival and her willingness to scratch the woman's eyes out if necessary, the butterflies in her stomach had never stopped their frantic flapping for fear he would be glad to see Suzanne again.

For a moment after turning in Mitch's direction, Suzanne remained frozen in place. Then suddenly, she let out a squeal and threw herself at his chest.

Emma raised an eyebrow as Mitch stumbled backward off the porch step, his arms flailing at his sides to keep from falling over.

"Oh, Mitchy, Mitchy, I missed you so much."

Suzanne's voice was high-pitched and saccharine-sweet. She kissed one cheek and then the other over and over again until Emma wanted to throw up.

"Suzanne." Mitch grabbed her wrists, finally managing to pry her hands from around his neck, and pushed her away. "What are you doing here?"

Emma wasn't sure, but she thought his tone held an edge

of irritation. She hoped so, anyway. She wasn't sure she would be able to handle it if she sensed he was happy about his ex-wife's return in any way.

"I missed you, Mitchy. I want us to get back together and be happy again."

"What about Kevin?"

"Oh, he's just an old pooh. I was an idiot for running off with him when I had you here to love me. Can you ever forgive me?"

Mitch was quiet for so long, a bolt of panic hit Emma in the solar plexus.

What if he did forgive Suzanne? What if he wanted her back?

Without any real intent in mind, she pushed the screen open and stepped onto the porch, letting the door close with a slam behind her. The noise sounded like a gunshot to her ears and caused Mitch's head to jerk up, his gaze to meet hers.

Releasing his hold on Suzanne, he moved around her and toward Emma. He climbed the porch steps, coming to a stop at her side and placed an arm around her waist, his hand resting on her hip.

"Suzanne, I believe you've met Emma. My wife."

Emma's heart swelled with pride at Mitch's pointed introduction, at the same time that relief made her feel lightheaded. He wasn't going to throw her over right here and now for his ex-wife.

The expression on Suzanne's face was nothing short of hateful—and aimed directly at Emma.

"I didn't know you got married again," she said with a distinct pout.

"You don't know a lot of things about me," Mitch retorted. "That's just one of the reasons *we* aren't married anymore."

Suzanne's arms took up residence beneath her breasts

again, thrusting them up and together, creating a bottomless chasm of cleavage that even Emma was having trouble tearing her eyes away from.

"Well, can we at least talk for a minute?" she asked, tapping one foot in frenetic agitation. *"Privately?"*

Emma stiffened at the sound of that. The woman couldn't be planning to say anything good if she wasn't willing to say it in front of Mitch's new wife, now could she?

Glancing up, Emma found Mitch staring down at her. His eyes were dark and hooded, giving her no clue as to his inner thoughts.

"Do you mind?" he asked.

Yes! she wanted to scream. Yes, she minded. Yes, she was insecure and frightened and beginning to feel territorial.

But, of course, she couldn't tell him any of that. Not without coming across as clingy and angst-ridden.

"No, go ahead," she answered, the words scraping past her throat like rusty nails.

He let go of her waist and started down the porch steps, following Suzanne as she sashayed her way across the lawn. They didn't go into the barn but stopped a few yards from the wide double doors.

Emma couldn't hear what they were saying, but she certainly noticed the number of times Mitch's ex reached out to touch him. The brush of her fingers along his arm, pretending to pick a piece of dirt or lint off the front of his shirt, leaning close enough for the tips of her breasts to brush his chest.

A twitch started at the corner of Emma's left eye, and she lifted two fingers to cover the stress-induced tick.

As she watched the couple with her good eye, she saw Mitch shrug, Suzanne give him a smug smile, then both of them turn and walk toward her. Suzanne headed for her car, climbing in and driving away without another word to either of them. Mitch continued on his path to the house, coming to a halt directly in front of her.

He stuffed his hands in his pockets and rocked back on his heels. "Sorry about that," he said. "I never expected her to show up here."

Emma gave a small nod, not sure how else she was supposed to respond. Then she cleared her throat and ventured, "So what did she want?"

His mouth turned down in a frown and he shook his head. "I don't want to talk about it right now. I'm going for a shower, okay?"

Without waiting for her to respond, he brushed past her and into the house.

She turned, watching as he walked away and did the math in her head.

Fourteen hours. For fourteen hours, she'd had an almost perfect marriage. She'd actually been happy and thought Mitch had been, too.

For fourteen whole hours.

Mitch stood under the hot spray of the shower, wishing the pelting droplets could wash away the last twenty minutes of his life.

Just when he'd thought things were going pretty well. He and Emma had worked out a truce of sorts, which he could only be grateful for. And they'd spent the night and half the morning making love like bunnies.

Maybe if he hadn't gone out to the barn. If he'd stayed in bed with Emma, maybe the entire day wouldn't have been ruined.

But, no, Suzanne had a way of ruining things no matter what.

God, why the hell did she have to come back? Why now?

Oh, but he knew why, thanks to the little "private chat" she'd talked him into out by the barn. She'd left her beloved Kevin, the man she'd been sleeping with while still married to Mitch, and was looking for a reconciliation. She claimed to want him back, to still be in love with him, to be sorry she'd ever cheated on and left him.

Of course, he didn't believe a word that came out of her mouth. Not anymore.

There'd been a time when he had believed her, trusted her. He'd been stupid, blinded by lust and convinced he was in love.

Now, he knew better. Love didn't step out on you, flirt with other men in front of you just to make you jealous, do its best to alienate you from your family in hopes of getting more time, attention and money.

Suzanne used to flash that sultry smile, toss her hair over her shoulder and run her painted nails down the middle of his chest, and his groin would take over the thinking process from his brain.

He shook his head in disgust, ducking once again under the pulsating spray.

The question was, what did she really want?

It was completely possible that Suzanne *did* want him back, he just didn't buy the reasons she'd stated—love, regret, second chances. No, she was up to something, and he had no intention of giving it to her.

But that didn't mean her visit hadn't stirred up old memories.

He scrubbed his skin hard with the bar of all-purpose soap, trying to wash off both the sweat and grime of the day's work, as well as the stink of his ex-wife's untimely appearance.

He'd thought he was over her, and in a way he was. He was over *her,* but apparently he still wasn't past the heartache and hard feelings she'd caused by her betrayal. Which only pissed him off more.

Damn her. He wished she'd stayed with her precious Kevin and kept the hell out of his life.

Shutting off the water with a jerk of the knobs, he climbed out of the shower and began toweling dry.

And then there was Emma. He knew she was upset about Suzanne showing up on the doorstep, and he hadn't helped matters by refusing to talk to her afterward. But he'd just wanted to get away, to be alone, to lick his wounds and do his best to drive his ex-wife's voice and image from his mind.

Now, though, he owed her an explanation. Or at least some reassurance that Suzanne wasn't going to become a permanent part of their lives. Not if he had anything to say about it.

Padding barefoot and bare-ass naked to the bedroom, he climbed into a clean pair of denims, threw on some socks and grabbed a fresh shirt, buttoning the front and cuffs on his way downstairs.

He found Emma in the kitchen, starting on supper. She had a cast-iron frying pan on the stove and was rolling chicken parts in a spiced flour mixture before dropping them into the hot oil.

Her fried chicken was one of his favorite meals, but tonight he couldn't seem to work up an appetite for it.

She turned her head when she heard him enter the room. Her lips lifted up at the corners, but the smile didn't reach her eyes.

"Feel better?" she asked, returning her attention to her task.

"Yeah," he responded, although it wasn't quite true. The shower had gotten rid of the dirt on his body, but he couldn't say he actually felt any better.

"Look—" he said, taking a spot opposite her and leaning against the countertop with his arms across his chest "—I'm sorry about the way I left things after Suzanne took off."

She shot him a sideways glance without pausing the movements of her hands as they flipped a thigh in flour. "That's all right, I understand."

Maybe that was the problem, Mitch thought crossly. She was too damn understanding. If he'd done something similar to Suzanne, she'd have pitched a fit, screaming, yelling, crying, chasing him around the house and possibly even lobbing something at his head.

But, ironically, Emma's lack of reaction annoyed him almost as much as one of Suzanne's rages would have. Didn't she care that his ex-wife had shown up out of the blue? That Suzanne had left her second husband and now wanted Mitch back?

A little bit of jealousy wouldn't be out of the question. God knew he'd been jealous enough to chew glass when he'd found Emma in his brother's arms. His own brother, whom he never really believed would make a move on a woman he knew Mitch was interested in.

But Emma didn't seem to be jealous of Suzanne at all, and, on top of everything else, that just put him in a worse mood.

"Well, just so you know, she won't be coming around again." At least he hoped not.

Emma nodded, still facing the other direction, showing no reaction whatsoever. If she was in a snit, she'd just have to get over it because he didn't know what else he could do or say to set things right. Suzanne's visit sure as hell hadn't been his idea, and he'd be damned if he was going to grovel over something he'd had absolutely nothing to do with.

"So…is there anything I can do to help?"

"You could set the table," she said without looking at him.

He pushed himself away from the counter to collect plates and utensils.

Good. Great. That was that, then. It was over and they could all go back to their lives.

But the hard knot in the center of his stomach as he set the dishes on the table and went back for paper napkins told him that wasn't the case at all. He had a feeling things between Emma and him were going to get worse before they got better.

Things could have been worse, Emma decided a couple of weeks later.

Her relationship with Mitch had never returned to the happy, euphoric state she'd thought they'd accomplished before Suzanne's reappearance in their lives, but it hadn't gone back to that cold place where they avoided each other and walked on eggshells, either.

They shared meals and talked more than they had during the first weeks of their marriage. Sometimes, they worked together, when Emma asked him to go over some papers or figures with her in his office or the few times he let her help him in the barn.

Of course, she knew darn well that he didn't really need her help and that the jobs he allowed her to do were simple, lightweight tasks meant to make her feel useful. But then, she didn't need him to help her with any of the ranch's paperwork, either. She only said she did occasionally as an excuse to be near him and as a way for them to do something that made them feel—to her, anyway—like a team.

And they slept together every night, in his bed. She'd abandoned the guest room and all but moved into the master bedroom with him, where they made love, whispered in the dark and slept in each other's arms.

It was almost, but not quite, perfect.

Mitch still didn't love her. She lived with that knowledge every day, and in her own way had made peace with it.

Her biggest fear at the moment was Suzanne...Yates Ramsey Burnes, who was doing her silicone-breasted best to become simply Suzanne Yates Ramsey again.

She'd been back to the house four more times since that first visit. Every couple of days she showed up, staring daggers at Emma while batting her lashes at Mitch and taking every opportunity to touch him.

To Mitch's credit, he tried to fend off Suzanne's inappropriate caresses and to make it clear he didn't want her around. But she was deaf to his protests—or pretended to be. And the fact that Mitch was remarried...that his new wife was standing not three feet away the entire time... didn't faze her in the least.

Emma could tell Suzanne's visits bothered Mitch. After each one, he became stoic and withdrawn, barely speaking the rest of the night, sleeping on his side facing away from her, making no effort to touch or hold her.

She tried not to take it personally. Suzanne had cheated on him, left him for another man. And now she was back. That was bound to put any man in a bad mood.

But she couldn't help being afraid that he was pulling away, that Suzanne's presence was beginning to put a wedge between them.

He told her he was over Suzanne, that he had no desire for the reconciliation his ex-wife was pushing for, but how could she be sure?

He'd been in love with Suzanne at one time, Emma knew that. Her betrayal had hurt him, and Emma didn't know if he was over it even to this day.

What if he was remembering the Suzanne he knew

when they were dating and first married? What if he thought they could make another go of it, that things would be different the second time around?

The very idea that she might lose him to his ex-wife sent a chill through her bones that settled around her heart.

If only he would take her in his arms and tell her she had nothing to worry about. That he loved her and felt nothing for his ex any longer.

But he couldn't tell her something he didn't feel. He might want her physically, care for her as a friend and the mother of his unborn child, but he didn't love her the way a husband should love his wife.

And that's what scared her the most. Because if he didn't love her, there were no emotional ties to keep him with her, and the chances of his being lured back to Suzanne were that much higher.

She did her best to hide her fears, to pretend everything was all right and not let him know she died a little inside every time his ex-wife's car rolled up the drive.

The baby growing in her belly was the only thing keeping them together, and even though he'd told her he wanted to do the right thing, give their child a name and the stability of a two-parent family, she knew perfectly well that if he decided to take Suzanne back, he could divorce Emma and still be a decent father.

He'd wanted to be with her when he didn't think he had any other options. But his ex-wife was definitely offering him other options. Two rather large, bouncy options that any man would be reluctant to pass up.

Emma heaved a disheartened sigh and set her mug of once-hot, decaffeinated tea on the kitchen counter. She'd wasted enough time today staring out the kitchen window at the barn, watching for any glimpse of Mitch as he went about his workday and wishing things could be different.

She had work of her own to do. And as long as she was still married, she might as well make the best of it.

Grabbing a banana from the bowl of fruit in the center of the table, she headed for Mitch's office…which was quickly becoming *her* office, since she was the only one who used it these days for anything more significant than piling more papers on the desk.

She plopped down in the wheeled leather desk chair and clicked on the computer, then took a bite of banana and started sorting through stacks of file folders while the system booted up. The files were bright orange, red, blue, yellow…she loved color and one of the first things she'd done after taking over Mitch's accounting and records was to replace all the boring manila folders with new, brighter ones. It also made organization easier, since she could co-ordinate all of Mitch's sales in red, purchases in yellow, bills in blue, et cetera.

Following her own system, she set aside the items she'd already worked on and tried to separate out the things that still needed to be done. As she twisted in the chair to set aside a stack of completed work, a large brown envelope slid off the desk and onto the floor.

She'd never seen it before, but that wasn't unusual. Mitch often laid "to do" stuff on the desk or on the small corner table just inside the door for her to deal with later.

The mailer was unsealed and unmarked, with no names or addresses to clue her in as to its contents. Reaching inside, she pulled out a sheaf of papers and began to scan the neat, printed words.

Mitch's name within in the paragraphs of legalese didn't concern her, since she figured it was just another piece of ranch business. Perhaps the sale or purchase of a registered steer.

But when her father's name caught her eye, her eyebrows knit and she slowed her quick skim to go back and read the document word for word.

The more she read, the sicker she felt. Her stomach cramped, and bile began to climb its way up her raw throat.

Oh, my God. No, it can't be true.

But it was right there in front of her, in black and white. And even though her vision was growing cloudier by the second, she wasn't mistaken in her understanding.

The document was a legal codicil to her father's will, leaving the Double D to Mitch upon Wyatt Davis's death.

And all Mitch had had to do to earn this prime inheritance was marry her.

Thirteen

Emma lurched to her feet, dodging furniture on her race for the kitchen, making it just in time to vomit into the stainless-steel sink. With her head spinning so fast she felt like she might pass out at any moment, she ran water to rinse the basin and her mouth and splash her flushed face.

Dear God. Her father had sold her like one of his brood mares. And Mitch had taken her on not because he loved her, not because he wanted to be married or wanted another wife, but because he stood to gain just short of a hundred acres of land that connected directly to his, as well as several head of cattle and horses.

She clutched the edge of the counter, letting the tears run down her face unchecked. In a flash, Mitch's first proposal and later his determination to marry because of her unexpected pregnancy came back to her.

The emotionless pitch, the press for responsibility, respectability.

Oh, he might have wanted to do right by his child, but she was sure her father's generous offer made it a much easier pill to swallow.

Her breath was coming in gasps, her lungs seizing painfully with each inhale and exhale of oxygen. She turned, still holding tightly to the countertop to keep from sliding to the floor, still blind to her surroundings. She heard the wracking sobs filling the room, but couldn't even register that they were her own.

With her arms stretched out on either side of her body, she took one lurching step after another, making her way to the staircase and up to the second floor.

She had to get out of here, had to get away before she went crazy. She couldn't be in this house another minute, knowing her marriage was a fraud…more than she'd ever believed possible. Knowing that Mitch had lied to her, betrayed her…*bought* her.

Stumbling into the guest bedroom, she grabbed an empty overnight bag from the closet and carried it with her to the bathroom and into Mitch's room, tossing in items she thought she might need to get through the next few days. Her toothbrush, some bras and panties, a couple of shirts and pairs of slacks. She didn't know where she was going, but she could buy whatever else she needed once she got there.

One thing was certain—she was never coming back to Mitch's house. She was taking herself and her child and getting as far away from him as possible.

Let Suzanne have him. Let the devil take him. She really didn't care as long as she never had to look at his lying, deceptive face ever again.

She wasn't going to her father's place, either. As far as she was concerned, he was just as guilty in this betrayal as Mitch.

How could he do this to her? Her own father!

Bag in tow, she hurried down the stairs, wiping her cheeks with the side of her hand. The screen door banged against its frame as she pounded across the porch and jumped in her car. She twisted the key in the ignition, barely waiting for the engine to sputter to life before putting the vehicle in gear and stomping on the gas.

Gravel spun up behind her rear tires, leaving deep tread marks along the drive. But she didn't slow down, didn't look back.

She was leaving Mitch Ramsey in her dust—literally and figuratively. Forever.

With a slight limp to his right leg, Mitch ambled slowly from the barn to the house. He'd had a minor run-in with an eight-hundred-pound bull this afternoon, but he counted himself lucky he was only sore instead of sporting a few broken bones—or a broken neck.

When he opened the front door, he expected to find Emma in the kitchen. It was almost dinnertime, and usually when he came in from the barn she was busy cooking and setting the table.

She would look up from whatever she was doing and smile at him. Ask about his day and how the new colt was doing. Then she would tell him supper would be on the table by the time he got back from his shower.

It all made him feel very…domestic, comfortable, safe. Instead of being a trial, having Emma in his house felt right. Having her in his bed felt even better.

He didn't want to think too much about that, about how well she fit into his life. Having her around was definitely a plus, and he didn't get that sick, panicky feeling in his gut anymore when he thought about being married again. With a kid on the way, no less.

But she wasn't in the kitchen and he didn't smell anything baking. Maybe she was in the office or upstairs taking a nap. Lord knew the pregnancy could make her tired and out of sorts from time to time.

As he kicked off his boots and passed through the living room, he thought about the fact that things would be just about perfect if his ex weren't making a royal pain of herself. No matter how many times or ways he tried to make it clear he wasn't interested—he was married again to another woman, for God's sake!—Suzanne just wouldn't take the hint.

A part of him suspected she wasn't hanging around so much to win him back as because she was hoping to tap back into his financial support. When she'd run off with her rich boyfriend, she'd no longer needed his paltry income. And she hadn't been eligible for alimony because she'd remarried so soon.

He thanked God every day for that small blessing.

But now Kevin Burnes had filed for divorce and Suzanne was about to be left penniless.

Of course, with him being married to Emma—and having no interest whatsoever in a reconciliation—Suzanne would never again have access to his bank account.

So now she had switched gears and was attempting to guilt him into giving her money. But Mitch had wised up to his ex-wife's manipulations—finally—and he had no interest in getting involved with her again in *any* way.

Besides, he had a family to provide for now. He couldn't waste his time, energy or money on a woman who had cheated on him and then dumped him the minute someone better came along.

Something Emma would never do.

His brow creased as he passed the office. The door was wide open, but Emma wasn't inside.

He started up the steps, ducking his head into the bedrooms before making his way to the bathroom. She wasn't there, either.

Still, he wasn't worried. She could have taken a drive over to her father's place or might just be out back, sitting in the sunshine. He'd look more thoroughly after he got out of the shower.

Twenty minutes later, he was damp but clean and dressed in fresh clothes. The house was almost eerily silent. There were no footsteps, no clanking of pots and pans as Emma worked in the kitchen, none of the inattentive humming he'd grown used to.

He padded down the stairs to the front door, glancing outside and noticing for the first time that Emma's car was missing. Well, that was it, then. She'd gone over to her father's or run into town for something at the store. He was surprised she hadn't left a note the way she usually did, but it was no big deal. She'd be back soon.

After an hour passed, his stomach was growling so loudly he made himself a sandwich and considered calling Wyatt to see if Emma was there. He didn't want to come across as too protective or controlling, though, so he waited.

Two hours later, the sun began to set and Mitch admitted that he was starting to get worried. It wasn't like Emma to take off without telling him. It wasn't like her not to call and let him know where she was or how long she'd be, especially when it started to get late.

Picking up the cordless phone, he hit the speed dial number for her father's house and listened to the ring on the other end while he paced though the house like a caged animal. Wyatt picked up on the third ring.

"Hel-lo?"

"Wyatt, it's Mitch. Is Emma with you?" he asked, cutting right to the chase.

Silence filled the phone line for several seconds and then Wyatt said, "No, I'm afraid she isn't. Is something wrong?"

"No," Mitch answered, cursing himself for causing Emma's father any premature upset. He should have called a couple other places first. "I'm sure everything is fine. Emma wasn't here when I came in from the barn and I didn't find a note. But I'm sure she just went out for milk or something. She probably got cornered by one of the town gossips and is still trying to make an escape."

He laughed, trying to lighten the mood of their conversation, but he didn't think Wyatt was buying it.

"Anyway, give me a ring if she stops by, but I'm betting I'll be calling you back in a few minutes to tell you she just pulled up the drive."

He said goodbye and punched the disconnect button, letting his arm drop to his side as he considered where else Emma might be. It was unlikely she'd gone to his folks' place without him, and he didn't know any of her girlfriends' numbers by heart.

"Dammit." He let his chin fall to his chest, pressing two fingers over the bridge of his nose where a headache was beginning to pound.

Where the hell could she be? It was one thing to visit a friend or run into town for a while. But she'd been gone for four hours now, and that was only since he'd come in from the barn. God knew how long she'd been gone before that.

An arrow of fear stabbed his heart, stopping him in his tracks. What if something had happened? What if she'd gotten sick or hurt? What if she'd started to cramp, gotten worried about the baby and didn't think she had time to find him before going for help?

He never should have left her alone.

Pivoting on his heel, he raced to the office, desperate to find phone numbers for all of Emma's friends and acquaintances. He would start with her obstetrician and call everyone in the phone book, if he had to, until he tracked her down.

Dropping down on the seat of the chair, he started searching the desk, opening and closing drawers in search of her address book. His hand bumped the computer's mouse and the monitor suddenly came to life. Which only increased his concern, since Emma tended to turn the computer off whenever she wasn't using it.

He hadn't found a paper address book, so maybe she kept her contact information on the PC. His hand was on the mouse, scrolling around to find his options when his elbow knocked a pile of papers to the floor.

He swore, long and harsh, leaning over to pick them up without taking his attention from the computer screen. As he tossed the papers back in the center of the desk, he caught a glimpse of the top page out of the corner of his eye.

They seemed familiar, and he paused for a moment to look at them more closely.

His chest grew tight and a sinking feeling began to slide through his gut when he realized what they were. It was the legal document Wyatt had given him right after he'd married Emma. The addendum to his will, leaving the Davis ranch to Mitch in the event of Wyatt's death.

They'd both signed it, and Wyatt had been as pleased as a cat who'd just dropped a dead rat on his owner's bed. While Mitch had been more uncomfortable, never thinking his agreement with Emma's father was really appropriate.

And now he knew his uncertainty had been a warning. He should have turned Wyatt down. He should have backed out of their deal when he'd had the chance or burned the damn papers the minute he got home.

He sure as hell shouldn't have left them where Emma might find them.

Because she had. She'd found them and read them, and now she thought he'd only married her for a parcel of land. Nothing could be farther from the truth, but she didn't know that.

How could she, when he'd done everything in his power to keep her at arm's length?

His shoulders slumped and he scrubbed his hands over his face. God, he'd really messed things up.

And the worst part was that he'd hurt Emma. Something he would never do intentionally. He'd rather cut off his own arm than hurt her.

She was one of the only people in his life who hadn't said "I told you so" after Suzanne's betrayal and abandonment. Everyone else had acted like he was the world's biggest pushover. But not Emma. She hadn't criticized or made him feel like a fool, she'd simply been his friend and supported him, regardless of his decisions or mistakes.

He had to find her. Had to make her understand before he lost her.

The desk chair rolled back and hit the wall as he pushed to his feet, his long strides eating up the floorboards as he headed for the front of the house. He grabbed his cell phone and the keys to his truck, then yanked open the door. His hand was already on the screen when he lifted his head and found himself staring into the heavily mascaraed eyes of his ex-wife.

"Dammit," he bit out. "What are you doing here, Suzanne?"

He didn't have time to deal with her right now. And on top of that, he just plain didn't want to.

"What do you think I'm doing here, silly? I came to see you."

Her overly sweet voice grated on his nerves. It always had. He didn't know why he hadn't realized it before now.

Deep down, a lot of things about his ex-wife bothered him. Her bleach-blond hair. Her tight clothes. The way she hit on every man in a ten-mile radius, even after they'd married. Her Tammy Faye Bakker makeup job and cheap, cloying perfume.

Maybe his family was right—he was the biggest pushover in the known world.

Or he had been. But not anymore. He had his head on straight now and wasn't going to be fooled by a pair of big boobs and a false grin.

He pushed the screen door open, forcing Suzanne to take a few quick steps back. Her car salesman smile slipped for a moment before she caught herself and pasted it back on.

"Where are you running off to in such a hurry?" she asked, mincing to keep up with him in her too-tight, too-high heels as he crossed the yard to his truck.

"None of your business," he said, yanking open the driver's side door and climbing inside.

"Let me make something perfectly clear. I don't want to see *you*, Suzanne," he told her, not bothering to beat around the bush. "We're divorced and have been for four years. We've got nothing to say to each other. I'm not sorry you left, and I'm not interested in getting back together."

"But, Mitchy—"

"No. No buts," he said, finally meeting her pampered hazel eyes. "I'm married to Emma now. I love her and we're having a baby. You're not welcome here, Suzanne, so don't come around anymore." He turned the key, listening to the big V-8 engine roar to life. "If you do, I'll call the sheriff and have you hauled away for trespassing. And if you think I'm joking…try me."

With that, he put the pickup in gear and peeled out of the yard, leaving his ex to come or go or rot, for all he cared. He just wanted to find Emma, *pronto,* and bring her home.

He'd told Suzanne he loved Emma, and it was absolutely true. He couldn't believe he hadn't figured it out before now.

That's why he'd been willing to marry her, even after the fiasco of his first marriage to Suzanne. Not because Wyatt asked him to or offered his land in exchange for wedding vows to his daughter, but because he'd been in love with Emma the whole time.

Oh, wild horses couldn't have dragged such an admission out of him. He wasn't sure he'd even realized it, consciously. But somewhere, deep inside, he'd known.

The question was, could he convince Emma of that before he lost her forever?

Flipping open his phone, he punched numbers with the side of his thumb while steering with one hand and trying to keep his eyes on the road. When his mother picked up, he got straight to the point, asking if she'd seen or heard from Emma. She hadn't, but promised to call him if Emma showed up.

Then he dialed his brother, hoping he was still home instead of off on another one of his high-powered business trips.

"Ramsey," Chase answered.

"Emma's missing," he said without preamble, knowing his brother would recognize his voice. "Is she there with you?"

"God in heaven, Mitch. When are you going to cut out the jealous, suspicious crap? You never used to be like this.

And it's starting to tick me off that you think I'd ever hit on or sleep with your wife…or any woman you were interested in."

"Chase," Mitch muttered between clenched teeth. "Shut up. I'm not asking if Emma is in your bed. I trust her a little bit more than that. And I trust you, too," he added, realizing it was the truth.

Emma would never cheat on him the way Suzanne had. She didn't have it in her. He suspected he'd known that all along or he never would have married her in the first place. Not even after he found out she was pregnant.

And if there was anyone he could trust as much as Emma, it was Chase. As brothers went, he'd gotten a good one.

"I'm calling because I'm worried about her, and I thought you might know where she was. I thought she might have come to you to tell you what a jerk I am."

"What kind of jerk are you?"

"The first-class, dumb-as-an-ox kind."

Chase chuckled, but his amusement fled as soon as Mitch told him about the deal he'd made with Wyatt Davis and the papers Emma had found in his office.

"Geez," his brother said with a long, drawn-out whistle. "Just when I thought you couldn't screw up any bigger than letting that blow-up doll, Suzanne, get her claws into you."

"Yeah," Mitch agreed, feeling his face heat with shame and embarrassment. "Not two of my finer moments, I'll give you that. But I love her, Chase."

"Who, *Suzanne?*"

The horror in his brother's voice made him chuckle, despite the concern coursing through his bloodstream.

"No, not Suzanne," Mitch told him with complete conviction. "Emma. I'm in love with Emma, my wife, and I don't want to lose her over some stupid agreement I made with her father that I never even cared about. Will you help me find her?"

"You know I will. Give me an idea of where to look."

Mitch didn't have the first clue, not if she wasn't at her father's. But he asked Chase to help him make some phone calls, and they divvied up areas of Gabriel's Crossing to search.

Then he hung up and began to pray. That he'd find Emma, and she and the baby would both be safe and healthy when he did. That she would give him a chance to talk, to explain, to beg forgiveness before she gave him the boot.

And that she would believe him when he told her he loved her.

Fourteen

An hour later, Mitch spotted Emma's car in the parking lot of the Dew Drop Inn on the outskirts of town, and stood on the brakes. His truck fishtailed for a second before he regained control.

He pulled in beside her at an awkward angle and jumped out. It was tempting to just start pounding on doors, or to take a guess that Emma's room would be the one directly in front of where she parked. But he couldn't be sure and didn't want to cause a scene or do anything to scare her unless he had to.

Marching to the motel lobby with its neon Vacancy sign in the window, he asked which room his wife was in, then had to provide proof of his identity before the teenager working the counter would tell him.

Lucky he hadn't burst through the door he'd first wanted to, because it turned out she was two rooms down. He found the number and lifted his fist to knock.

When no one answered, he rapped again. "Emma? Emma, it's Mitch. I know you're in there. Open the door. Please."

"Go away."

His heart swelled at her response and a wave of relief washed through him. She was here and she was all right.

But just as quickly, his stomach clenched at the sound of tears in her voice.

He laid his palm flat on the flimsy wooden panel and rested his forehead on the ridge of his knuckles. "Emma, honey. Open up. Please? I want to talk to you."

"Well, I don't want to talk to you. Go away or I'll call the front desk and tell them you're harassing me."

A muscle along his jaw ticked as he gritted his teeth in frustration. How was he ever going to apologize and make her understand if she wouldn't even let him in?

"Dammit, Emma, open this door right now or I'll kick it in. All I want to do is talk to you. If you don't like what I have to say, I'll leave."

Silence met his plea.

"All right, here goes," he said, taking a step back and readying himself to follow through on his threat. "One…"

Still nothing.

"Two…"

He heard a muffled "Fine" and then the chain on the other side jingled. The door opened with a squeak and Emma stood there staring out at him, her face pale, her eyes red and swollen from what he suspected were hours of crying.

Her obvious misery hit him like a punch to the gut, and he wanted to fall to his knees right then and there and beg forgiveness.

She crossed her arms, emphasizing the sexy swell of her breasts and the rounded paunch of her adorable pregnant belly.

"Are you all right?" he asked, needing more than anything to know she and the baby were okay. Then he shook his head. "I know you're not all right. I know you saw the papers for the agreement I made with your father. But I mean physically. Are you and the baby okay?"

"We're fine," she said grudgingly. "But I'm not coming back with you. I'm leaving. I'm filing for divorce and taking the baby, and I never want to see you or my father again."

He knew it was her hurt and anger talking, but her words stabbed straight through his heart.

"Don't do that," he said, his own voice low and scratchy with desperation. "Please, just listen to me."

Reaching for her wrist, he moved forward, forcing her to walk backward farther into the room. He kicked the door closed with his booted foot, telling himself he deserved her wariness when she pulled out of his grasp and shot a fearful glance over his shoulder at her only mode of escape.

"I know you hate me right now, and you have every right. I hate myself for what I've put you through. But I'd like a chance to explain. Please."

Her arms went back across her chest and she took a defensive stance a few feet away. "There's nothing you can say that will ever make up for what you and my father did."

Moisture gathered on her lashes, twisting his insides.

"You're absolutely right. You can't know how sorry I am about that. But you have to believe me when I tell you that I don't care about your father's ranch. He came to me with this bizarre proposal to leave the Double D to me in his will, as long as I became part of the family by marrying you. And I don't think he did it because he was in some all-fired hurry to marry you off. He was more concerned about the land ending up in the wrong hands, afraid you wouldn't want to run things after he passed.

"And I agreed because…" He took a deep breath to slow his racing pulse and garner courage for what he was about to say. "Because I love you."

He'd expected her to doubt him at first, but he hadn't expected the snort and eye-roll that accompanied her skepticism.

She sniffed and grabbed a tissue from the bedside table to wipe her nose. "Right. I'm supposed to believe that the man who accused me of cheating on him with his own brother and then wouldn't touch me after we were married was *in love* with me."

"Would it help if I told you I'm an idiot?"

"No. I already knew that."

A smile tugged at the corners of his mouth. Moving slowly so he wouldn't spook her, he stepped forward and took her by the arms, steering her in the direction of a worn vinyl chair.

"Sit down for a minute. Please."

For a moment, she looked like she might argue but then did as he asked. He lowered himself to one knee in front of her so they were eye to eye.

She was so beautiful, so precious to him, and he'd royally screwed up his chances of keeping her.

If he lost her now, he didn't know what he would do. Cry like a baby. Stop breathing. Crawl into a hole and die of loneliness. All those options held some appeal, since living without her would be no life at all.

"I'm an idiot for a lot of reasons, but the biggest is that I let Suzanne's betrayal make me think I could never trust a woman again. Which is complete hogwash. I could always trust you. I knew it, even if I wasn't willing to admit it.

"I didn't think I could handle the pain and humiliation of marrying another woman only to have her cheat on me, too. And the best way to keep something like that from happening, I thought, was to shut down, cut myself off. Pretend I didn't want or feel."

He wrapped one hand lightly around her wrist, feeling the pulse beating there, rubbing his thumb back and forth across the delicate veins beneath her skin.

"But I did want—I wanted you. And I did feel—I felt so many things for you, they scared me. *That's* why I agreed to your father's asinine plan, Emma. Not because I was interested in the land, but because I wanted you and didn't know how else to get you, keep you. Your father's offer gave me an excuse to marry you without having to admit that I felt something for you.

"And then when you told me you were pregnant..." Covering her expanding stomach with his free hand, he let his head fall forward until their brows met. "God, I was so happy. But I was petrified, too. I'd done such a thorough job of cutting myself off from my emotions, I wasn't sure I could turn them on again enough to raise a healthy, happy child. But I wanted to try. And it seemed like the perfect opportunity to bind you to me. Legally. Forever."

He leaned back, searching her damp, lovely blue eyes for some sign that she was listening and might be willing to forgive him.

"Don't be angry with your dad, baby. Please. His intentions were good, even if he went about them in a very bad way. And don't hate me, either. Please. I love you so much, it feels like my heart is going to explode if you leave me.

"I know I don't deserve it, and I have no right to ask, but give me a second chance. Come home with me and let me prove to you that I'm telling the truth. We'll tear up that damn codicil, burn it in the fireplace. Then we'll go over to your father's and do the same with his copy. And I told

Suzanne to leave us alone or I'd have her thrown in jail, so she shouldn't bother us ever again."

Seconds ticked by while he kept his gaze locked on her face, his chest tight with panic and the effort to draw air into his lungs.

"You hurt me, Mitch." Her bottom lip trembled and tears spilled over her lashes to run down her cheeks. "You really, really hurt me."

Gathering her close, he wrapped his arms around her and let his fingers tangle in the fall of her hair. "I know, sweetheart. I'm so sorry. I never meant to. I'd rip out my own heart before I'd hurt you on purpose."

She sniffed against his shoulder and he felt a small shudder roll through her fragile frame. He squeezed her even tighter, afraid that if he let go, if he loosened his hold for even a minute, she would slip away from him again.

"I'd like to tell you I'll never hurt you again, but I've still got that idiot thing going for me, so chances are, I will. The best I can do is promise you that I'll try not to. And if I do, you can tell me. You can hit me, beat me, yell at me. Just don't leave me."

He ran his hands through the hair at her temples, loving the soft texture of it against his skin. Then he gently kissed one corner of her mouth, followed by the other.

"Don't leave me, Emma. Stay with me and be my wife, my lover, the mother of my children. Help me run the ranch and show the folks of Gabriel's Crossing that even though I was stupid enough to hook up with the wrong woman once, I finally wised up and married the right woman. The only woman I could ever love."

She pulled back a little, and for a moment he was afraid she was going to turn him down. That his words meant nothing and he was going to lose her, anyway.

"Do you really love me?" she asked in a low voice.

He answered immediately, relieved to finally be able to express his feelings for her. "More than my own life."

"Would you really have married me, even if my father hadn't made that ridiculous offer? Even if I hadn't gotten pregnant?"

"Yes. It probably would have taken me a while to figure out that that's what I wanted, though—" he made a face "—since we've already established that I'm not the brightest bulb in the lamp when it comes to that sort of thing."

A soft smile started to curl her lips. "No, you're not. I've been in love with you since I was a little girl, and you never once looked at me like you might feel the same."

He pulled back, stunned by her admission. He didn't know what to focus on first—the fact that she'd said she loved him or that she'd had feelings for him longer than he'd ever imagined.

"Did you just say you love me?" he asked, wanting to be one hundred percent sure.

She nodded, lifting her own arms to fan her fingers through his hair and across his scalp. "Since we were kids. Then you went and married that bimbo and broke my heart."

Her grasp on his head tightened and she gave him a little shake. "No more bimbos," she told him sternly. "No more stupid deals with my father or anyone else, and no more pretending you don't care about me. If we're going to make this marriage work, then you have to be honest and open with me and stop punishing me for your *ex*-wife's behavior."

The hard knot of worry that had taken up residence in the pit of his stomach began to loosen as her meaning sank in, and his grin felt like it was about to split his face.

"Yes, ma'am."

"And you have to tell me you love me at least once a day. Twice if you do something idiotic."

He laughed, enjoying the vibrating sensation in his chest and moving up his throat. It had been too long since he'd laughed, too long since he'd been truly happy.

"Yes, ma'am." He would tell her a dozen times a day, if it would make her happy. Hell, it would make *him* happy.

"So will you come home with me?" he asked, not ready to completely abandon his fears until he heard her say the words.

"Yes, I'll go home with you. *After* we stop at Pop's to rip up those damn papers."

He chuckled again and hugged her close, pressing his lips to her ear, her throat, her cheek until he reached her mouth.

"Deal," he whispered and sealed it with a kiss.

Epilogue

The Dixie Chicks crooned about wide open spaces over the stereo speakers set up on either side of the big white gazebo in the center of the park, while couples danced and children chased each other through the grass, screaming and laughing. Everyone in Gabriel's Crossing had come out for the Fourth of July celebration, bringing their best covered dishes and dressing in red, white and blue from head to toe.

Emma smiled at Ida Mae Fisher, who was telling her yet another story about one of her fifteen grandchildren, and nodded at what she hoped were appropriate intervals, But her gaze scanned the crowd, looking for two familiar faces.

Her husband, who had gone off about an hour before to play a game of horseshoes, and her three-month-old daughter, who was being passed around like a bowl of mashed potatoes at Thanksgiving dinner.

It was the baby she was most concerned about. Amelia was so little, still a newborn, practically, and Emma didn't deal well with having her daughter out of her sight. Never mind that it had been her mother-in-law who'd taken the baby from her arms or that the woman had raised two children of her own.

She was a nervous, overprotective mama, Emma thought. So shoot her.

Two large, masculine hands snaked around her waist, locking in the middle and making her jump. She tilted her head back to find Mitch's gray eyes and grinning lips only inches away.

"Good lord, you scared me," she said, giving his arm a light swat.

"Ida Mae," he drawled in that whiskey-smooth voice that made her spine go soft and tingly, "would you mind if I borrowed this pretty young lady for a minute? She's needed over by the dessert table."

The older woman's eyes crinkled at the corners and she waved them away. "Of course not. You two go on. I'll finish telling you about little Dwight Allen later."

"Oh, goodie," he whispered in her ear, keeping his tall body pressed against her back as he turned with her and walked them both in the other direction. "I'll be sure to get you back for the rest of that story."

She chuckled. "That's all right. I can live without knowing how they got the kernels of corn out of his nose. Thank you for rescuing me, by the way."

Instead of leading her to the long picnic table weighed down with cakes, cookies, brownies and pies, he steered her away from the festivities toward the field of parked cars.

"You're welcome. I really did need to talk to you, though."

Her amusement fled in a rush, replaced by an immediate flicker of fear. She stopped in her tracks and twisted to face him, forcing him to halt, too.

"What's wrong? Is it Amelia? Is she sick? Did she get hurt?"

"The baby's fine," he answered patiently before she could break away and go in search of their daughter herself.

A second later, he'd neatly maneuvered her between two vehicles so that her back was against the passenger side door of his big blue truck. He leaned in and took her mouth, kissing her until her toes curled and her bones began to melt.

When he lifted his head, they were both breathing rapidly and she'd forgotten what she was worried about only a moment before.

"There. Now will you stop worrying about Amelia?"

"I'm a new mother. It's my job to worry."

His face split into an understanding smile. "I know. And you're very good at it."

She raised one eyebrow.

"At being a mother, I mean," he added quickly. "Not the worrying part."

"That's what I thought you meant," she said, letting him off the hook with a grin of her own.

"So what do you say we sneak away from the party and go home, where we can be alone for a change and fool around like teenagers. There's a new litter of kittens up in the loft I've been meaning to show you," he added as extra enticement.

Her blood warmed at memories of their first night together, in the loft of her father's barn, and at the thought of being alone with him again. Really, truly *alone*.

Since Amelia's birth, it seemed like their house had been overrun first by well-wishers dropping in to bring gifts and get a glimpse of the new baby, and then by

Emma's father and Mitch's parents, who were playing their roles as grandparents to the hilt.

And after everyone else finally left, either Amelia still needed their almost constant attention or they were just plain exhausted.

"I'd love to," she said.

They'd been at the town picnic three or four hours already. She was more than ready to go home for some peace and quiet. And if she was lucky, maybe a little cuddle time with her husband.

"Let me just collect Amelia and we—"

Mitch covered her mouth with his own and kissed her into silence once again.

Mmm, she rather liked his method of shutting her up. If he ever tried it during an authentic argument, she'd probably have to deck him, but as an every day mode of hushing her up it was certainly something she could get used to.

"When I said 'alone,' I meant it," he explained when he broke off this time. "Just the two of us. My mom's going to keep Amelia for the night."

Emma shook her head, already suffering the first twinges of separation anxiety. "Oh, no. I couldn't—"

"*Yes,*" he stressed, "you can. You need to. We both need to."

Before she could protest further, he brought two fingers up to her lips. "Amelia is going to be fine. Mom and Dad are thrilled about having her all to themselves, and you know they'll take nothing but the best care of her. I already put the car seat and diaper bag in their car, and I made them swear that if they needed anything, they'd call. I'll keep my cell phone on me at all times," he added, wiggling his eyebrows suggestively. "I may even set it on vibrate."

"Very funny." Biting her lip, Emma looked back over

her shoulder at the throng of people, not seeing Theresa and the baby, but knowing they were there somewhere.

"Come on," Mitch cajoled, his hot breath fanning over her cheek and neck as he lowered his head to nibble at her throat. "Say yes."

Her maternal instincts warred with the lust and need coursing through her veins. Finally, common sense won out.

Amelia would be fine for one night. And she really did miss being alone with Mitch, just the two of them, to do all the naughty, sexy things that had brought them together in the first place.

"All right," she acquiesced, her fingers curling into the firm muscles of his upper arms as his tongue did wicked things to the lobe of her ear.

She could feel the tilt of his grin in the curve of her shoulder, and then he gave her a tiny nip before straightening to meet her gaze.

"Have I told you yet today that I love you?" he asked.

As always, those three words coming from him made happiness burst inside her.

"Yes, you did. This morning, over breakfast."

"Hmm." His eyes narrowed as he studied her. "Well, I'm going to say it again, just in case I've done something stupid, or do before the day is out. I love you."

She chuckled, wrapping her arms around his neck and lifting up on her toes to reach his mouth. "I love you, too. But don't worry, you've been a very smart man lately."

"The smartest thing I ever did was marry you."

The conviction in his voice and sincerity shining in his eyes made her want to weep. She tugged him close and kissed him to let him know just how proud she was of the changes he'd made, leaving all of his hang-ups and insecurities over his ex-wife behind him.

And then he was shifting her to the side, opening the truck door and lifting her onto the seat. A second later, he'd rounded the hood and climbed in behind the wheel.

Emma smiled, taking in every detail of her husband's profile as he drove them home faster than the law allowed.

They'd come so far in one short year, overcome so much pain. But she wouldn't change a minute of it, because in the end, she'd gotten everything she'd ever wanted.

She'd gotten Mitch.

* * * * *

New York Times *bestselling author*
Linda Lael Miller
is back with a new romance featuring
the heartwarming McKettrick family
from Silhouette Special Edition.

SIERRA'S HOMECOMING
by Linda Lael Miller

On sale December 2006,
wherever books are sold.

Turn the page for a sneak preview!

Soft, smoky music poured into the room.

The next thing she knew, Sierra was in Travis's arms, close against that chest she'd admired earlier, and they were slow dancing.

Why didn't she pull away?

"Relax," he said. His breath was warm in her hair.

She giggled, more nervous than amused. What was the matter with her? She was attracted to Travis, had been from the first, and he was clearly attracted to her. They were both adults. Why not enjoy a little slow dancing in a ranch-house kitchen?

Because slow dancing led to other things. She took a step back and felt the counter flush against her lower back. Travis naturally came with her, since they were holding hands and he had one arm around her waist.

Simple physics.

Then he kissed her.

Physics again—this time, not so simple.

"Yikes," she said, when their mouths parted.

He grinned. "Nobody's ever said that after I kissed them."

She felt the heat and substance of his body pressed against hers. "It's going to happen, isn't it?" she heard herself whisper.

"Yep," Travis answered.

"But not tonight," Sierra said on a sigh.

"Probably not," Travis agreed.

"When, then?"

He chuckled, gave her a slow, nibbling kiss. "Tomorrow morning," he said. "After you drop Liam off at school."

"Isn't that…a little…soon?"

"Not soon enough," Travis answered, his voice husky. "Not nearly soon enough."

REQUEST YOUR FREE BOOKS!

2 FREE NOVELS PLUS 2 FREE GIFTS!

Silhouette® Desire®

Passionate, Powerful, Provocative!

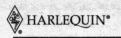

HARLEQUIN®

American **ROMANCE**®

IS PROUD TO PRESENT

COWBOY VET
by Pamela Britton

Jessie Monroe is the last person on earth
Rand Sheppard wants to rely on, but he needs
a veterinary technician—yesterday—and she's the
only one for hire. It turns out the woman who
destroyed his cousin's life isn't who Rand thought
she was. And now she's all he can think about!

"Pamela Britton writes the kind of
wonderfully romantic, sexy, witty romance
that readers dream of discovering
when they go into a bookstore."

—*New York Times* bestselling author
Jayne Ann Krentz

Cowboy Vet *is available from*
Harlequin American Romance in December 2006.

nocturne™

**Explore the dark and sensual
new realm of paranormal romance.**

HAUNTED
BY LISA CHILDS

**The first book in the riveting
new 3-book miniseries, Witch Hunt.**

DEATH CALLS
BY CARIDAD PIÑEIRO

**Darkness calls to humans,
as well as vampires...**

*On sale December 2006,
wherever books are sold.*